# THREE ACROSS KANSAS

By the Same Author

*Three Across Texas*

# THREE ACROSS KANSAS

Jack P. Jones

Walker and Company
New York

All the characters and events portrayed in this story are fictitious.

First published in the United States of America in 1986 by the Walker Publishing Company, Inc.

Published simultaneously in Canada by John Wiley & Sons Canada, Limited, Rexdale, Ontario.

Library of Congress Cataloging-in-Publication Data

Jones, Jack Payne, 1928-
Three across Kansas.

Sequel to: Three across Texas.
I. Title.

PS3560.04885T44 1986 813'.54 85-29493
ISBN 0-8027-4059-6

Printed in the United States of America

10 9 8 7 6 5 4 3 2 1

*For Ronald*

# THREE ACROSS KANSAS

# CHAPTER 1

IT nearly killed us. When we crossed the Red out of Texas, we owned two good horses, a mule, a solid wagon, ample supplies, and the clothes we were wearing. Upon reaching the Kansas border, we had only a tired mule, few supplies, and dead men's clothes on our backs.

The late-afternoon air held a chill as we made camp at a small stream under the cottonwoods. In the distance, the dozen or so buildings of the Kansas border town were just a defenseless blotch on a wide stretch of rolling prairie. It had been four weeks to the day since we forded the Red River into Indian territory.

Sooey removed the pack from the mule and took his ax to gather firewood. Sis began taking things out to fix supper. I swung the barrel of the Winchester .44 across my shoulder and went back up the slope. I knew he'd be on our trail. He was always out there—the old man and that wolf look-alike dog.

Sis searched me with large, blue eyes when I returned to where she was putting on the beans. She removed her wide-brim hat, letting her hair fall down over her shoulders. A sun ray darted through the tree branches, sparkling against the black strands.

"Jonah?"

"He's still out there."

She looked toward the town, her hands on her hips. The Colt .45 strapped around her slim waist seemed to weigh her down.

"By damn, we made it, Jonah!"

"Now the fight really starts."

She looked at me. Her round, smooth face, tanned by the

sun and wind, was no longer the face of a girl. She was an eighteen-year-old woman—all five feet three inches of her.

"We'll kill them the same as we did that other trash," she said slowly, perhaps remembering how the three of us came close to being the ones to die.

My sister was three years older than me. I suppose that could account for her being more sure about things.

The clothes we wore were taken off dead men: white renegades who tried to kill us back in the Nations. The horses, the wagon, and most everything else were taken by the band of Indians before the whites came upon us. One of the braves wanted to take Sis. I had levered the rifle and aimed at his nose. Sooey had picked up his ax and stood in front of Sis. I think it was the size of Sooey and the ax that caused them to have second thoughts.

We'd followed the Chisholm Trail across that wild country. I'd wanted to wait and travel with one of the cattle drives that would be coming along later, but Sis decided we'd start out around the first of March.

The worn denim pants and black coat were much too large for Sis. The tattered black hat with the wide brim drooped down in front, causing her to tilt her head back whenever she wished to look straight ahead. But the good part about being dressed the way she was was no one could tell she was a woman unless they were up close. She was careful to keep her hair pushed up under the hat.

Sooey returned to camp carrying an armful of firewood. The brown-striped pants he wore were too tight and stopped about four inches above the tops of his shoes. We couldn't find a coat he could get into, so Sis cut a hole in the center of an old green blanket and pulled it down over his head.

Hats were not made large enough for Sooey. The nearest thing to a fit was a black derby that sat on the top of his head. It was constantly falling off until Sis made a tie-string for it. Sooey kept the string under his chin even when there was no need to. He thought it was what Sis wanted him to do. He'd do anything for Sis.

It'd been some time since Sis had given him a haircut, so his yellowish hair hung down over his ears. Sooey claimed he'd been to a barber only five times in all his twenty years.

His square face was a big grin when Sis thanked him for the firewood. Childlike gray eyes searched the top of a cottonwood and he chuckled, taking deep breaths. He lifted the corner of his blanket-wrap and stuck the ax handle under the wide belt he wore for that purpose. Sooey considered himself well armed with that big, double-edged ax. I suppose he was.

He came over to where I was watching the rim of the rise behind us. Though he was better'n six feet six, he actually appeared short until he was towering over you. Being so broad and thick probably caused the illusion. His arms were nearly as big as my thigh.

"Thister told me. . . ." He paused, searching for a word. ". . . we have one can of peaches left." He grinned.

I looked up at him, having to lean back to do so. "I like peaches," I said.

"Me, too, Jonah. You—you can have my thare."

I had to smile. Folks back home claimed Sooey was simple-minded, but I never thought he was as stupid as they believed. His biggest problem was that he couldn't pronounce an *s*. When he tried to, his tongue wouldn't work just right. "No. We go equals on the peaches," I said.

A huge hand gently squeezed my shoulder. He hurried back to the fire to help Sis.

My clothes didn't fit no better'n Sis's. There had not been a slim man in that bunch that attacked us. The brown pants were too big and I had to shorten the length of the legs with my pocket knife even though I measured a good five feet ten when I stood straight. The coat was a darker brown than the pants and nearly wrapped around me twice. Like most Fletchers, I was as thin as an Ozark rooster. I'd rolled the sleeves up a turn so they wouldn't interfere with my handling the rifle. I still had my old black wide-brim. The bullet hole in the crown was of no matter.

The reason we were nearly naked when the bank of white scavengers attacked us was that the morning before, the Indians made us give them the clothes we wore—leaving all of us in our longjohns, including Sis.

Pa'd said that Sis took after Ma's side—mostly fire and thunder—while I took my looks after the Fletchers. Big ears and nose ran in the blood. The Fletchers all had light brown hair. I was the only Fletcher Pa knew who had such a cowlick. The only way I could comb my hair was from one ear straight over to the other. Sis said it made me look stupid.

Sis's nose sort of turned up at the end. She thought it was ugly and would fight you if you made an unkindly remark about it. Actually, I thought Sis was pretty, even if she didn't. When she had on clothes that fit, no one could mistake her for a boy—not even at a distance, though I don't recollect ever seeing her in a dress.

We sat down on the ground to eat. I stood the rifle against a tree where it'd be handy. We had ample rations of beans and hoecake. Later, Sis would divide the peaches.

"Looks as if we'll have to walk across Kansas," I said.

Sis had a mouthful of beans. "If we walked all the way across Texas and halfway through the Nations, we can surely make it across Kansas. Anyway, Abilene's really not that far."

"You think they'll be there?" I said.

"We'll find them. If not there, then some other place. Abilene's where the herds go. That's where the money is, and if they're not there, they'll be somewhere close."

"Just two more to go and it'll be finished," I said to no one in particular.

Sis stared at the fire. "Just two more, Jonah."

Six men had raped and killed our older sister and shot Pa to death. Four of them were dead. Now we intended to make the other two pay. We had settling to do.

Oates Smith and Marvin Hollend were the last surviving members of the Soltz gang, the ones who had visited our ranch in south Texas and committed the deed. Sis had seen the whole thing. Hiding in the loft, she saw Soltz and his men drag Pa and Hester into the barn that afternoon. She'd watched them beat and shoot Pa, then rape and kill Hester.

"Just two more," she said again.

Sis divided the peaches and we ate them slowly, wanting to make them last. Night crept over the prairie. A cool wind rustled the leaves of the cottonwoods and I listened, wondering about the man who'd been following us. The thoughts of that big, gray dog slipping up on me in my sleep sent cold chills up my spine.

"That man out there," I said. "Maybe he knows where we're going and why."

"Could be, Jonah," Sis allowed. "Word spreads over a thing like what happened in Timber Creek. Soltz was gunned down face to face by a fifteen-year-old with a rifle. Folks talk about things like that."

I'd been scared and I didn't like to think about it. I hoped I would never be put in such a position again. Sis almost got me killed!

"We find them," Sooey said, chewing the last of his peaches.

Sooey had been on his own since he was a small child. His mother died, leaving him to beg for a living in Mesa Flats, a small town in south Texas. Most everyone in the town laughed at him but me and Sis. He was a good friend and very loyal. I was glad he'd decided to travel with us on our mission.

The hobbled mule munched grass noisily nearby. A coyote wailed somewhere far off. Downstream, a frog croaked a protest as if the pungent fragrance of our campfire irritated him. A nearly full moon rested on the horizon.

I picked up my rifle and started up the grade.

"Be careful," Sis warned.

He was an old man, thin and of medium height. I could see that much the night I had slipped in close to his camp a few weeks before. The short white beard was the only part of his face I had seen. The dog began growling. The old man had reached out and placed a hand on the animal's thick neck.

"If you were Injun, this dog would have already killed you," he said easylike. "Now you get along, boy. Our time will come soon enough."

He didn't look up nor make any attempt to reach for the long double-barreled shotgun leaning against the rock ledge behind him.

He was out there tonight, as always—a ways off, camped under a clump of small trees—perhaps on the same stream that flowed by our camp. It was a good fire. He hadn't made any attempt to hide his presence, nor had he tried to harm us—yet. Who was he and what did he want? Why would an old man be following us?

We'd tried to lose him, but he stuck to our trail like an Indian. About all we knew was that he walked with a limp, favoring his left leg.

Of course, there was that dog. . . .

*"Our time will come soon enough."*

What did he mean by that?

When I returned to camp, Sis poured a cup of coffee, handing it to me. Sooey, with his back against a tree, bit off a chew from a plug of tobacco.

"He's out there, ain't he?" Sis asked.

"Like always."

"Well, we've more important things to think about than some old man. This is Kansas and we'd better keep alert."

Sis's real name was Katrina. I thought it sounded pretty when spoken slowly. I stretched out on my blanket, listening to the frog.

"Ka-tri-na," I said softly.

She was fussing with her blanket, having spread it out over some small stones. She sat up quickly.

"What!"

"Do we have enough money to buy a wagon?"

"You know we don't. We might have enough to keep us in supplies if things go well."

"Reckon those people in town are friendly?"

"We're not going in there to make friends! We buy our supplies and get out."

They were not the least bit friendly. It was a border town accustomed to outlaws, killings, and general lawlessness. There was not a lawman within fifty miles.

Sooey led the mule with Sis walking beside him. I followed a short ways behind, carrying the rifle in the crook of my arm.

Most of the buildings were mud-chinked logs. A couple soddies had shingle roofs. The saloon, however, had board siding.

"Who's the big squaw under the blanket?" someone chided from one of the stores.

We paid him no attention, continuing down the street toward the mercantile.

"Them clothes they're wearing look familiar," a man in the bunch gathering in front of the saloon said.

We walked on.

"Hold up there!" another demanded, stepping out into the street.

He wore a bushy mustache and he hadn't shaved in several days. A Smith and Wesson .44 pistol protruded from his waistband. Even though he was dressed like a ranch hand, I knew better. Probably the town bully. He was large enough to force his way on folks.

"Boy, that coat you're wearing belonged to a friend of mine! I'd recognize that patch on the sleeve anywhere."

I had turned to face him, still holding the rifle in the crook of my arm. Sis and Sooey waited behind me, to my right.

"Where'd you get that coat, boy?"

"Off a dead man."

"Where?"

"Down in the Nations."

"Who killed him?"

"I did." I was able to keep my voice calm, without trembling.

"You shoot him in the back, boy?" he demanded to know.

"Didn't have to. He was facing me same as you are."

"You're a liar!"

"There were others with your friend. Four, to be exact," I said, my voice still managing properlike. "They tried to kill us."

"And where are they?" Seemed like he was trying to snarl.

"Likewise dead."

"Backshooters!" he growled, moving his right hand toward the butt of the Smith and Wesson.

I quickly levered, twisting so the rifle pointed at his chest. Pa'd taught me how to rifle. He'd claimed I had a natural gift; that I was a born rifler.

The bully looked down the barrel of my .44. His hand dropped to his side. "There'll be another day, boy."

"There always is," I said, glad he'd backed down. No one else in the group took it up, so we moved on down the street.

Sooey tied the mule up in front of the store. "We'd better get our supplies and get out of here," Sis warned. "I don't think he liked having to back off from a boy."

"I'm fifteen!" I reminded her.

"I know you're almost full-grown, Jonah. I just hope you don't have to prove it to them."

I sat on a bench in front of the store. "I'll keep an eye on the mule while you and Sooey do the tradin'," I said.

I took off the wide-brim and wiped a sleeve across my damp forehead. Three men rode into town and dismounted in front of the saloon.

I wasn't full-grown. Dangerous men frightened me. I wanted to get the killing settlement done with so Sis, Sooey, and I could go somewhere and live without the fear of being shot or knifed.

Pa began teaching me to rifle when I was eight. I didn't know then that one's legs turned to mud when facing someone who wanted to shoot you.

When they came out of the store, each sucked on a peppermint stick. Sooey tied the two sacks of supplies on the mule. Sis handed me a candy. When we started out of town, the saloon emptied. The bully and the three men who'd just ridden in spread out in the street.

"Trouble, Sis," I warned.

We stopped. They were a good fifty yards away. Unless they were experts with pistols, I had the advantage. Pa always claimed that a pistol-shooter didn't stand a chance against a rifler at such a distance.

They seemed undecided. I was hoping they'd pass it off as just a little fun, but I knew different.

"Jonah?"

"I see him."

The old man rode in, walking his horse up the street. The dog followed at the heels of the big, black horse. Across from the saloon, he dismounted and limped up the steps to the porch of the café.

The bully and others must have wondered about the long ten-gauge resting on his shoulder as he leaned against the post. I know I did.

The dog stayed with the horse, looking at me. He was the meanest-looking four-legged creature I'd ever seen. The hair all along his back stood straight up.

The man standing next to the bully took two steps toward us, standing straddle-legged like he was preparing for a draw-down. He wore a Colt .45 in a holster tied to his leg. About the same size as the bully, he had a wide face with sunk-back eyes. He was of a kind you always expected to smell—and usually did. Even at a distance.

"They call me Gage," he said, trying to sound important. "I'm known as a fair man and I usually have the last say around here."

Out of the corner of my eye, I saw Sis ease back her coat and rest the palm of her hand on the butt of the Colt. That was when they realized she was a woman. Gage grinned.

"Tell you what I'm gonna do, kid," Gage called out. "You

folks are wearing clothes that belonged to my friends. You strip them off, bring them here, drop them at my feet, and you can leave."

The group at the front of the saloon laughed.

"I'll strip the girl, Gage," the bully said.

"The last son of a bitch who tried that is lying face down out yonder on the prairie!" Sis snapped.

"You the law?" I directed at Gage.

He was looking at Sis. "Some folks think I am. Girl, it's up to you. You can save them. Strip off them clothes and bring them here!"

"You got a badge?" I asked.

He patted his holster. "This is my badge." He was still staring at Sis. "Girl?"

"I'll strip her, Gage," the bully announced, starting toward us.

I brought the rifle down and fired when it leveled his chest. The bullet kicked him back. When he fell, he never moved again.

I worked the lever, throwing another cartridge into the chamber. I flipped the barrel back to rest across my shoulder.

"My sister warned you," I said. "Now, you can bury that bastard!"

Gage hesitated. "Who the hell are you?"

"His name is Jonah Fletcher," the old man said slowly from across the street. "That's the trio that cleaned out that hell hole called Timber Creek last fall."

The onlookers moved back against the saloon. The old man chuckled. "You want to undress the girl. Go ahead. He's just a kid. Shouldn't be no big task for three hardcases. But I gotta warn you. That big 'un under the blanket may not be any too bright, but he can kill a man with his fist."

He chuckled again. "Come here, Sweetie."

The dog growled, curling lips to show fangs. The hair along his back remained straight up. He stalked toward the old man, grumbling low in his throat.

He kept up the menacing sound while standing beside the old man.

"Go ahead, Gage," he said. "Strip that little gal naked. Of course, she's the one who sent that knife-cutter Beaumont to hell. First, she shot him point-blank in the belly with that peacemaker she's totin'. Then, when he was on his knees, she shot off half his face."

He was chuckling. The dog threatened. "But you go on. Finish what you started."

"What's your part in this, old man?" Gage demanded.

"Know'd you'd ask that. Sweetie, what's our part in this?"

The dog went bare-fanged into a crouch, ready to leap to attack.

"Sweetie says that's something we'll have to wait and see about. You going to make that boy's sister take off her clothes or not?"

Gage turned to go into the saloon. "I'll have my day soon."

"Stay put!" Sis demanded.

Sooey and I followed behind as she walked toward them. I held the rifle ready.

"By damn, since you're so set on undressing folks, you do it! Take off your clothes and pile them in the street."

"The hell I will," Gage said.

"Sooey," Sis said. "Hit him!"

Sooey did. He smashed a big fist against Gage's mouth, bursting lip and loosening teeth. Gage hit the ground sliding on his rear.

"Get on with it!" she ordered the two standing.

One let his hand touch his gun. I pointed the rifle at his face.

"I was just gonna drop it!" he cried.

"Better do it with the buckle," I cautioned.

They both unbuckled their gun belts, letting them fall.

"Bring me some coal oil," Sis told the saloon woman standing on the walk.

The woman hurried into the saloon. She returned with a lamp. "Will this do?"

It was half-full. "It'll do," Sis said. She turned to Sooey. "Get that trash to his feet, Sooey."

Sooey jerked Gage up. Sis removed his gun, pitching it over into the water trough. "You've got a choice, Mister Last Say. Either you can strip or Sooey'll do it for you!"

They undressed down to their underwear and threw the clothes in a pile.

Sis poured coal oil on them. "The underwear, too," she ordered, turning her back.

"Now look—" Gage started to protest.

"Sooey," Sis said. "Help him out of his longjohns."

Sooey started for him. They stripped off their longies in a hurry and pitched them on the pile.

"Now, you walk down the street and out of town," she said, her back still to them. "Jonah, shoot the first one who tries to run."

"My day'll come," Gage said tightly, his sunken eyes flaring. "We'll meet again. That I promise you!"

Standing there without any clothes on, one could not, at the moment, work up much fear of him.

"Best you get to walking," I said.

While they didn't break out in a jog, it didn't take them long to make it out of town. There were a few onlookers and snickers along the way too.

Sis set fire to their clothes, and I looked around for the old man. He was gone.

"Ain't no need looking for him," the saloon woman advised.

"Who is he?" Sis asked. "He's been following us for a ways now."

The woman looked at Sis and then at me, the hard lines on her face drawing tighter. "I don't know. But he has the look of death about him. And that beast he calls a dog could be Satan himself."

She pulled Sis's coat open, looking at her closely. "There's a lot of woman hid under these rags," she said casually. "All full-bloom and tender. Gage knows that. In his mind, he's already stripped you bare. He'll not rest until he's had you naked and raped. Then he'll kill you for what you just did to him. He'll make it as painful as he can. He's got more men. Tough men. They're off raiding someplace, but they'll be back in a day or two."

Sis jerked her coat from the woman's grasp.

"I wouldn't trade places with you, honey." The saloon woman shook her head. "With none of you!"

# CHAPTER 2

THREE days later, we made night camp early, feeling better now that there was distance between us and the border town. The old man still trailed us, stopping when we stopped, moving when we moved. I wondered why he didn't just have it out with us, whatever his business was. It was damn peculiar, this game of his.

My shoes were wearing thin, my nerves thinner. It was the dog. I felt cold chills whenever I thought of him. The old man and his shotgun didn't give any comfort either. I decided to put the whole business out of my mind and joined Sis and Sooey at the narrow creek.

They were sitting on a log with their bare feet dangling in the water. I did likewise, keeping my hands on the rifle.

"Jonah, I get cold chills all over when I think about that old man and his dog," Sis said.

"It's a pretty dog," Sooey said, splashing a big foot about. "I like the way he growls."

Sis looked at me. I shrugged. Sooey also liked screaming panthers and grumbling bears.

"One thing's for sure," Sis went on. "The old man knows all about us."

"Seems so. Oates Smith and Marvin Hollend probably know we're coming for them."

"If they do, they'll be prepared and waiting, Jonah." She tilted her head back, looking at me from under the wide-brim. She was worried and so was I. Sometimes, I wondered if I'd ever reach sixteen.

"But we'll think of something, Jonah," she said. "You'll see. It'll turn out just fine."

She always said that when she was more worried than she let on.

"It'll be fine," Sooey added, splashing with his other foot.

Two frogs downstream started an argument. It was cool under the trees, refreshing and comfortable. The little creek moved along slowly. What sounded like a wolf howled out on the prairie. Likely as not, it was Sweetie. I felt cold all of a sudden.

"Ka-tri-na?"

"You teasing me again, Jonah?"

"No."

"Jonah, you know something? I was real scared back at the border town when I thought we might really have to undress."

"So was I."

She looked down at the water. "I was really frightened," she added softly.

"I know."

"No, you don't. I—I didn't have on any underwear," she whispered so Sooey wouldn't hear.

"Not even your shorties!"

"Ssshhh!" She smiled slightly, looking at me out of the corner of an eye. "That could have been terribly embarrassing, don't you think?"

"You would have been naked!"

"*Ssshhh!*"

"You would have been naked," I whispered.

"You already said that."

Sooey looked up at the treetops, splashing both feet.

Sis's eyes sparkled. The little grin around her mouth warned me to be on the watch for trickery. "That saloon woman said I was full-bloom and tender. Do you think so, too, Jonah?"

"I don't know about the tender part."

She looked like she was ready to run a pout. "I am blossomed some, Jonah. I nearly pop the buttons on this old shirt."

"Breasted better'n most," I said before thinking.

"Really?"

"Fletcher women run that way, according to Pa."

"What about the rest of me? Am I filling out like I should?"

"Heck, I don't know, Sis. When you're wearing clothes that fit, you look well enough. I don't know much about girls and such." I put my shoes on and picked up the rifle. "I'm going to look about some."

"I'll get to fixing supper."

Sooey jumped up. "I'll get wood, Thister."

"Jonah?"

I turned around. Her eyes seemed bluer than ever. "If something happens, Jonah . . . if we don't make it . . . I want you to know, you make me proud."

"We'll make it, Sis. And I think you're full-bloom *and* tender."

We were camped along a creek at the bottom of low slopes. I climbed the incline, sat down, and waited. The shadows of dusk moved in. Soon, I saw the flicker of the old man's campfire. It was nigh smokeless as always.

Then I saw the thin trail of smoke in the distance, beyond the old man's camp. Whoever it was didn't try to hide their presence.

Returning to camp, I filled my plate with beans and fried salt pork. I told Sis about seeing the smoke.

"Could be Gage and his band," she said, concerned.

She sat on the blanket next to Sooey and ate in silence. When she finished, she began gathering things.

"Leave the fire burning. Sooey, pack this stuff on the mule. Jonah, go up and take another look."

"What are we going to do?" I asked.

"Find a place where we can fight!"

"There's trees here to hide behind."

"That's just it. There are too many trees. They could move right in here, jumping from behind one tree to the other until we're surrounded. Now, go up there and take a look."

"Can't tell much from up there, Sis. We might not find a place as good as this one," I said.

"There's a ghost town west of here, Jonah. I overheard the storekeep talking about it. Be a good place to make a stand."

"We might not find it."

"That's a chance we'll have to take."

"We find it," Sooey said.

Sis patted his arm. Red-faced, he turned around, looking the mule squarely in the face.

"You fill the canteens, Sooey?" she asked.

"Yes, Thister."

She led out. Sooey followed, leading the mule. I dropped back, bringing up the rear. Sis'd purchased a couple extra boxes of .44's back at the border town, so we had an ample supply of ammunition. The cartridge loops on her belt were full and there were two boxes of .45's in the pack. Since no one ever knew what a mule would do, I carried extra cartridges in my coat pockets. A man had to think ahead. Anything on the back of a runaway mule wouldn't do you a lick of good.

We moved on in the dark. Thunderheads had been gathering since late afternoon and now lightning began to play along the horizon. Seeing that no one was following us, I caught up with Sis.

We plodded along in silence, hoping that over the next hill we'd see the town. Distant thunder rumbled now and then. The wind blew hard.

Around midnight, we paused for a rest at a stream. The mule watered thirstily and we drank from one canteen. I refilled it.

Toward daybreak, Sis paused, studying the ground. "What's that look like to you, Jonah?"

"Old wagon ruts."

"To the ghost town, I bet."

"Could be," I admitted. "But which way?"

"We might be able to tell from up there," she said, pointing to one of the higher swells. "By damn, Kansas doesn't do anything but roll up and down, does it?"

"I like Kansas," Sooey said, grinning.

From the top, we saw the old town about a mile away, deteriorating in a vast expanse of grassland. We headed that way.

Most of the buildings had sod roofs as well as walls. One of the six structures across the wide street had a board front. Two fake windows were in the part that extended above the roof. It was a false front of sorts.

We decided to make our stand in the soddy at the end of the street. The walls were thick and the roof reasonably solid. With a door on the front and a small window in the back, we could cover two approaches.

Sooey untied the pack and dropped it in a corner on the packed-dirt floor. He tied the mule in the roofless log structure across the street. Sis then put him to work with his ax, making a slot in each of the soddy's end walls.

The black clouds still hugged the eastern skies. "Maybe it'll rain and cover our tracks, Jonah."

"I'd rather it didn't. If they're after us, I'd as soon get it over with."

"Well, in that case why not get a fire going and I'll make some coffee."

"Sounds fine to me," I said, looking about.

"And peaches, too!" Sooey pleaded.

Sis took a can of peaches out of the pack, and Sooey hurried off to find firewood.

She built the fire out front, a few feet from the door, and put on the coffee while I kept an eye on all approaches to the town. No one could slip in without my seeing them. We had a fair chance should an attack come.

It came at midmorning. Gage and seven riders, following our trail, walked their horses toward the town. I slipped around behind the building and entered through the window. Sis had put out the fire a short time ago, so they had no way of knowing which building we were in. That could work in our favor.

Pa wasn't a talkative man, so whenever he did say something, I listened. On one occasion, he talked about such an event as this; where he was holding up in a cabin with outlaws approaching. I tried to recall his advice. My heart pounded so hard I was afraid Sis would hear it.

*"Shoot to kill, son. Always make each shot a fatal one. Take your time. Don't panic. If you have to shoot some son of a bitch twice to kill him, then you're rushing it."*

I wiped a sleeve across my forehead. They were at the end of the street.

"Search out every building," Gage yelled. "I want that girl alive, you hear?"

All but Gage dismounted. They spread out, searching. Sis cocked the Colt. Sooey brought out his ax.

"Sis, you watch through that slot," I said, trying to sound calm. "Sooey, you guard the window. If a hand, gun, or head shows, use your ax on it."

"I will, Jonah."

"They're moving this way," Sis whispered.

"Let them come," I said, not knowing anything better to say.

Gage was holding back, staying close to the end building.

*"You have to take out at least two before you give away your position. Otherwise, you've lost the advantage of surprise, son."*

They were coming closer.

"Jonah?"

Two, holding cocked pistols, approached the place where the mule was tied. The .44 caught the one in front under the armpit and slammed him against the wall. Before the other could turn, I levered and hit him below the shoulder.

Sis fired through the slot and a man let out a scream that ended in a gurgle. At the window, an old outlaw showed his face, trying to find a target in the shadowed room. Sooey slammed the broadside of the ax into the face, smashing it.

Up the street, one made a dash through a doorway. The Winchester kicked against my shoulder and the bullet smashed his leg. He screamed as he hit the floor inside.

Gage and the two others let us have it, pinning us down with rifle fire. We stayed away from the openings.

"Where's Gage?" Sis wanted to know.

"I don't know. One is on the roof across the street. Another is inside that store with the one shot in the leg."

"Then Gage must still be down at the end of the street," said Sis.

Bullets dug into the rear wall, whizzing by my ear. Sis hugged a corner.

"Don't kill the girl!" shouted Gage. "She's mine!"

The firing slowed to silence. "Hey boy," yelled the shooter on the roof. "Your sister ain't hurt, is she?"

Sis peered through the slot, the Colt ready. I wiped my hands off on my pants. My mouth felt desert-dry.

"Know what we're going to do with your sister, boy?" he taunted, listing in vulgar terms what they planned to do. His words were filthy even for an outlaw.

Sis covered her ears. Sooey started to rush out with his ax. Sis grabbed him.

"It's all right," she soothed. "Jonah'll get him!"

"Thoot him, Jonah. Thoot the thonofabitch!"

*"Don't let the enemy force you to do something stupid, son. Keep your head. Act with reason. Not anger. Angry men are easily killed."*

The rooftop shooter began repeating his filthy barrage. I concentrated on watching the store. I knew there were two of them inside and even though we'd wounded one, he could still use a gun. A rifle muzzle appeared at the window. At the same time, a lanky fellow dashed out the door.

I aimed just above the barrel, easing pressure on the trigger. All the while, obscenities from the roof filled the air. When my rifle kicked, I didn't wait to learn if the bullet took him out. I dove through the door, landing on my belly. The tall man could run, I'd allow him that much. He was making a dash for the corner of our soddy.

In the instant he saw me come out the door, he tried to change directions and swing the rifle on me. I levered two quick ones. The first bullet went just wide, and I could've cursed, but the second took off the top of his head.

A bullet from down the street kicked dirt in my face. I made a fast crawl back into the soddy as fire poured from the rooftop.

Shoving fresh cartridges into the Winchester, I watched the rooftop for some movement.

An eerie quiet fell over the ghost town. We waited. It could be that Gage and Foul-mouth were doing some counting. My guess was that they were the only ones left. A drop of sweat fell off the tip of my nose. I wiped my forehead with my sleeve.

"Jonah?"

Sis beckoned for me to hurry. Running to the window, I saw Gage making a run for his horse at the rear of a building. He mounted, untied the other horses from the old corral fence, and set them running with a shout and a wave of his hat.

Swinging his horse around, he intended to send some farewell rifle shots at us. I fired too quickly. My bullet hit his arm, almost knocking him out of the saddle. Dropping the rifle, he grabbed for the saddlehorn with his good hand and raked spurs against his horse. The animal lunged, making a run after the other horses.

The shooter on the roof began screaming for Gage not to leave him, cursing all the while.

Going to the door, I levered. "Looks like you're all alone," I called out.

A pair of upraised hands showed first. Then he stood up. His revolver was still in the tied-down holster.

"Don't shoot, boy! I quit!"

Stepping out into the street, I swung the barrel of the Winchester over my shoulder, finger through the trigger guard. I moved down where I could face him. Sis and Sooey followed.

He must have been about thirty. His pale eyes flickered from one to the other of us. It struck me that he was as vulgar as his language. He stood on the roof, wide of hips and narrow-faced.

"Here I am," Sis snapped. "What was it you wanted with me?"

He tried to laugh.

"Drop your hands," I said as well as I could with a dry mouth.

"Now, boy. I already gave up," the thin voice whined.

"The hell you did!"

He tried to laugh again, holding his hands higher. "You can't shoot me like this!"

"I can," Sis retorted. "I'm the bitch you were going to spread-leg—among other things." She pulled the Colt.

He dropped his hands slowly, a sly look on his face. "I'm fast, boy."

"Good for you."

He made his move. My bullet ripped at his filthy mouth, knocking him into a somersault as it lifted him off the back side of the roof.

Sis wiped my forehead with her bandanna. "As soon as we finish supper, we'll leave this place," she said.

"I'll build a fire," Sooey advised hurriedly. He was always hungry.

Night moved in while we were eating. By now I wasn't surprised to see the smoke from a campfire just a little ways outside the town. Not surprised, but damn annoyed—and nervous. *If I could just get my hands on that old man,* I thought, *I'd shake it out of him. What the hell does he want with us?*

Sis was watching me and read my thoughts. "You might have to kill that dog, Jonah."

"I don't think anyone could kill that dog without being killed first," I said.

Later, we broke camp and headed in the direction of Abilene, knowing that regardless of when or where we traveled, the old man and his Satan dog would be with us.

# CHAPTER 3

WE approached the dugout cautiously. It jutted out from the side of a hill above the brush-lined stream. The front, a crude stacking of logs, had a door on leather hinges and a rifle port near each corner. A girl, wearing a gingham dress ripped at the shoulder, was in the small corral milking a cow. The cow's tail whipped across her face as she looked up.

Sis removed her hat. The girl came to the gate. "My goodness! Visitors this time of the year?"

She smiled, her green eyes shining. Her hair was as red as the hot coals of a campfire. You could tell she had been down at the stream scrubbing herself not too long ago. She not only looked clean but smelled soap-fresh. I judged she was about seventeen, filled-out and bouncy.

"My, my," she exclaimed when Sis introduced her to Sooey. She took his hand. "You're big as a giant!"

Sooey chuckled and searched for a hawk overhead.

Her name was Jane Placker. I felt my face burning when she reached for my hand.

"Oh my," she said, looking me straight in the eye. "You do stand straight and proud."

I took my hand away and she looked down at her bare feet. "When you finish growing, Jonah, you'll be right tall."

"I reckon."

I found myself helping Sooey search for the hawk. The way she grabbed at my eyes with hers was discomforting. Her skin was pinkish, looking as smooth as a new gunstock. Her nose was a trifle large, but that never took away from good looks.

"My, my," she said, casting her eyes on me.

She quickly turned to Sis. "Well!" she said, reaching for her hand. "Don't just stand out here. Come on to the house."

Sis turned her head to wink at me. I shrugged.

Her pa was lying on a bunk behind an old canvas separating his bed from Jane's bunk. He was dying. He said as much. We hadn't been in the dugout thirty minutes and already we'd promised to take Jane with us to her uncle in a town eighty miles to the north.

"We'll take care of her, don't you fret," Sis told him.

He looked like death, coughing all the time. His eyes went from Sooey to me. They rested back on Sis. "Fletcher, you say?"

Sis nodded. He coughed. "There's a family of Fletchers north a ways. Tough as a hickory stump and all rifle shooters."

"Kinfolk," Sis admitted, proudlike. Pa'd told us all about Uncle Harlan and his bunch of boys. We Fletchers weren't known to tolerate a lot of foolishness. Uncle Harlan was less accommodating in that respect than most Fletchers.

"You'll be safe with these folks, honey," he told Jane. He examined Sooey again. He towered over the bunk like a blanket-clad buffalo. "You won't let nobody harm her, will you?"

"No, thir!"

He managed a smile. "Honey, set supper for these folks."

There wasn't much there to eat. Sis sent Sooey out to get the pack and put the mule in the corral. When he returned with the pack, Sis took out beans, salt pork, flour, coffee, and peaches. Sooey grinned. I began cleaning my rifle and Sis's Colt.

"You good with that rifle, Jonah?" Jane asked, her voice like music to my ears.

"Fair."

"I can shoot, too," she advised, making biscuits. Whenever I looked up, she'd smile. She sure had a fetching way about her.

When supper was cooking on the hearth, Jane took the water bucket off the shelf near the door. "Someone had better go with me," she invited. "It's getting dark out."

"Jonah?" Sis said, focusing on me from the corner of her eyes.

I reloaded the Winchester and hung the barrel over my shoulder. "Reckon I'd better."

We walked toward the stream. It wasn't really dark. The sun was just going down behind the horizon, sending trails of red streaks across the sky. Jane's hair glowed.

"How old are you, Jonah?"

"Nearly sixteen," I stretched some.

She smiled, her full mouth parting over even, white teeth. "I'm just slightly over sixteen," she said, unstretching some. "My, my. I bet you'll surely grow another foot yet."

"We Fletchers grow tall," I volunteered.

She dipped up a half a bucket of water and turned to go. I took the bucket and dipped it full. A man ought not do anything halfway.

She held the handle, her hand touching mine. We carried the bucket between us, back to the dugout. We didn't say anything. Nothing needed to be said.

After supper, I stepped out with my rifle, the cool wind penetrating my worn coat. Millions of stars, some twinkling, stretched across the heavens in layers.

I breathed deeply, glad to be out of the dugout and away from the dying man and the daughter who suffered with him but tried to hide her sorrow. I'd seen her looking down at him, silent tears trickling down her cheeks. Long, red hair partly hid her face, but I knew what she was feeling. It hurt when Pa and Hester died. The hurt never stops.

The old man was camped aways down the stream, his fire a tiny glow through the small clump of trees. It seemed like every night he made his camp a little closer to us. I wondered if that meant anything.

*"Son, no one does anything without a reason. If you know the reason behind someone's actions, then you're one step ahead of him. If you don't, you're a mile behind. Hidden motives are often dangerous. Beware when a man's actions aren't clear."*

Jane came out to the corral, where I was checking on the mule.

She pulled the shawl closer around her shoulders. "Sis told me about him," she said, looking toward the old man's camp.

"She tell you about the dog?"

She shivered. "I hope he doesn't come up here!"

We leaned against the corral. I thought she was standing closer than necessary. I didn't mind, though.

"May I hold your hand, Jonah?" she whispered softly.

I swallowed as her hand slid into mine. It was callused some but felt nice and warm.

"My, my."

Throat lumps are aggravating. They make a man feel inadequate. After a while, I cleared mine, but it didn't do much good. Another one just come up.

"Jonah, what are you thinking?"

I shrugged my shoulders.

"We've got almost the same big nose," she said after a while. "I hated my nose until today when I saw yours, and then I was happy I had it."

"My pa used to say the reason we Fletchers could smell trouble so far off was because we had a nose for it."

She laughed. It sure was a pleasant sound. The old mule nudged the cow away from the trough and chomped on a ear of corn.

In a minute, she took my hand and pressed it against her face. Then she touched it to her hair.

I shifted my weight to the left leg. The right one nearly gave away.

"Am I embarrassing you, Jonah?"

"Of course not!"

"Ssshhh!"

"What were we talking about?" She wanted to know after I shifted weight again.

"Noses."

She reached up and ran the tip of a finger down mine. "My pa said a big nose meant strong character."

"I don't know. I know some folks with big noses and they don't have any character at all."

She leaned her head against my shoulder. I shuffled awkwardly and we moved off toward the house in silence.

That night her pa died. We buried him down under a cottonwood not far from a bend in the stream, a place where he used to go to spend time alone. Jane stayed at the grove while we readied to leave.

Later, she gathered her few things, wrapping them in a blanket. Sooey tied it on the back of the mule along with the pack, and we moved out.

When we reached the top of the hill, Jane stopped and looked back. The wind whipped her skirt. She held her bonnet on with both hands as she took a last look at the place. We waited. Soon, she wiped her eyes and turned, motioning us to move on.

We made good distance the next two days, seeing neither person nor house until we neared Newtown, a town with buildings on both sides of a sizable creek. Some of the stores had board siding. A footbridge crossed the creek about middle ways of the town. A false-front saloon stood on each side of the creek. Down a ways, a blacksmith hammered iron on an anvil. A few trees grew along the creek bank.

Sis said she needed sugar to sweeten our coffee, so we headed for a store. It was late Saturday afternoon and folks were coming to spend the evening in town, some in wagons, some on horseback.

Folks stared at us. The day was cool. Sooey had on his warm blanket, and the little derby was securely tied on. Of course, he wore his ax. I tried to talk him into putting it with the pack, but Sooey wouldn't hear of it. Sis had given him that ax and he wouldn't part with it for anybody. He even slept with it.

Sis's coat was buttoned, and being as long as it was, it covered the holster. I carried the Winchester across my shoulder and some gave it a hard look.

It had belonged to Pa. The octagon barrel had an adjustable rear sight of Pa's own design. The stock was of some special wood with golden swirls and streaks. The wide butt plate was brass, which I took pains to keep polished. The breech was engraved with Pa's name, Latin words, and a goddess of some sort. The rifle held seventeen cartridges. A rancher in Texas had handed the rifle to Pa as a gift. I never knew why. The day Pa and Hester were murdered, the rifle was in a gunsmith's shop having the firing pin replaced. If the Winchester had not been in the shop, Pa and Hester would still be alive.

Jane had not seen a town in two years, so Sis bought us all soda pop and we sat on a bench under a cottonwood to let Jane catch up with her looking.

Later, after we'd eaten and Jane was satisfied she'd seen enough, I went for the mule and we started out across the prairie. Sis dropped back to where I kept an eye on our back trail. "Something you ought to know, Jonah. Jane doesn't want to stay with her uncle. She wants to remain with us."

"Huh?"

Without looking, I knew Sis's head was tilted back, her blue eyes peering from under the wide-brim, trying to find something in my face she could later use against me. I was glad it was dark. You had to keep alert when Sis was about.

"By damn, Jonah! Is that all you going to say?"

"I'm thinking on it."

Sis hated my saying that, but it was the only way I knew to get thinking room.

We hurried along, keeping up with Sooey's long stride.

"Ka-tri-na?"

"What!"

"It's too dangerous. We've settling to do. At best, our chances of living through it are slim. She stays with her uncle."

She touched my arm. "I know, but I wanted to hear you say it."

We walked on. "Jonah?"

I stopped. She touched my arm again. "There's something else you should know. I think she loves you."

"I'm only fifteen. I'm just a boy!"

"She said you were man enough for her."

"Huh?"

# CHAPTER 4

I AWOKE with a start. It was just turning daybreak. As I brought the rifle around, the blurred movement was gone, disappearing through the thin brush. I knew what it was, though.

Sis stirred, then sat upright. "Jonah?"

"It's all right." I stood up, the rifle ready.

She stood up too. "What was it, Jonah? Tell me."

I paused. "That Satan dog," I said. I figured she had a right to know.

Sis sat down quickly. She turned pale. Her hands trembled. It was my fault. It was the first night we hadn't taken turns keeping watch. We'd been too tired to fret about it. I should have known better.

Sis gathered herself and stood up. Jane stirred under the blanket. Sooey snored loudly.

"I'll get something cooking," Sis said. "Sooey, get a fire started."

Sooey jumped up. "All right, Thister."

Jane came to life. She immediately set to work, getting things from the pack. I left to take a look around.

At a wide place at the water's edge, I found his tracks, the huge prints deep in the soft, damp earth. They appeared again on the bank across the stream. No dog could jump that far. But he must have! If he'd hit the water, I would have heard it.

Finding myself shivering, I went back to camp. I was beginning to believe Sweetie was more ghost than real. I wasn't even sure the old man was real, the way he appeared and disappeared.

The early sun was warm. We took our time with breakfast.

While no one had mentioned it, everyone knew that the settlement where Jane's uncle lived was just a few miles away. No one was in a rush. It was going to be a lazy day—a long one if we had our way about it.

Sis and Jane walked off toward the creek. I poured myself another cup of coffee. Sooey bit off a chunk from a tobacco plug and contemplated the fire, the coffeepot, the trees and the sky, spitting when the thought occurred to him. Most of the time, he just swallowed the juice.

"Keeps away belly worms," he'd once remarked.

Sis returned. She went over to the edge of camp and sat on the trunk of a fallen tree, drying her hair with an old shirt.

"Jonah."

I went over and sat beside her. She studied me, curiously. "It's time we discussed something."

I waited. She fussed with her hair. "I'm going to say it right out. There's no other way." She kept her voice down, not wanting Sooey to hear. "That all right with you?"

I said it was.

"You ever see a naked girl?"

"Huh?"

"Well, have you?"

"A naked girl!"

"*Ssshhh!*"

I tried to figure ahead of her. Something was about to put me in a mess.

"Well?"

"I'm thinking on it."

"Jonah!"

"Sis, I ain't never even seen a little naked baby!"

She fooled with her hair some more. "It's time you found out what a woman looks like."

"I know what a woman looks like."

"Not a *naked* woman, you don't!"

"I will someday," I said. "Besides, I saw you almost naked once."

She stopped messing with her hair. "When?"

"Last summer when you went swimming in that water hole outside Timber Creek."

"I had my underclothes on!"

"Well, that's almost naked."

"Jonah!" She slapped my arm hard.

She worked on her hair some more. I didn't see how it could get any drier. "Now you get on down to the creek, Jonah."

"Huh?"

"Go on. Get down there."

"Why?"

"Because there's a woman down there and she's bare-rump and pretty!"

"Jane's at the creek *naked?*"

"Ssshhh!"

"Suppose she sees me?" I whispered.

"There are plenty of bushes for you to hide behind. Go on, now."

I started off.

"Jonah."

"Huh?"

"Don't walk down there whistling."

I wished I knew what was ailing Sis.

I don't know what I was expecting to see. I had an idea or two about what a woman looked like. We Fletchers ain't stupid. But I nowhere near expected what I saw.

It bothered me a lot. I don't mean I was pained any. I sat down behind the bush, staring at the prettiest thing I'd ever seen.

She didn't have a stitch of anything on. Standing near the bank in ankle-deep water, she held her head up, letting the long, glistening red hair fall back over her shoulders.

Her body was the same pinkish tint as her face. Her breasts were full and thrust out, with nipples that made my mouth water. She had longer legs than I'd expected and I would never have guessed a girl's buttocks could be so round and smooth.

She turned slowly, facing my direction. My heart raced madly. She bent over and splashed water on her face and body. She stood up quickly, shivering. I wanted to dash out there and wrap myself around her.

She moved slowly toward the middle of the creek, where the water came up to her thighs. When she dipped down, only her head was out of the water. Then she disappeared.

She reappeared quickly, slinging the hair out of her face with a quick twist of her head.

The sun sifted through the branches. Coming to the bank, she stood quietly, watching a pair of birds chatter through their mating ritual. Her right side was toward me and I could only stare and swallow lump after lump. Actually, I had trouble breathing.

She took a deep breath and began dressing.

When she left, I went to lean against a tree. I felt drained and weak-legged. When the pounding in my chest and head had eased, I walked back to camp.

"You all right?" Sis asked.

"I will be—in a month or so."

She snickered. Jane was sitting under a large tree down a ways from camp. I started that way.

"Don't be long, Jonah," Sis said. "We have to be going soon."

I sat down beside her. She took my hand, leaning her head against my shoulder. "I'm going to miss you, Jonah."

I didn't say anything.

"Will we ever see each other again after today?"

"Maybe sooner than you think."

She drew back, green eyes sparkling. "Really?"

I nodded.

She jumped up, going to stand behind the tree. I followed. She pulled me against her, her arms going around me. "Kiss me, Jonah!"

I right away pressed my mouth against hers and smacked her good.

"My. Oh my," she sighed.

We kissed two or three times more. She squirmed against me and I held her as tight as I could, both arms squeezing.

"My goodness!" She breathed heavily and we went to kissing some more.

I had to force myself to back away from her. She turned her back to me, taking deep breaths. "My, my. Much more of this and we'll start a grass fire!"

She whirled around, unsnapping the front of her dress. She grabbed my hand and thrust it inside against one round, firm breast. Her hot breath fanned my face.

I swallowed. I couldn't speak. She held my hand there. She pulled up her dress and put my other hand on her backside. She didn't have on any underwear.

"Hold me tight, Jonah," she breathed into my ear.

I did.

Slowly, she moved my hand around to her front, pressing her softness against my palm. Her mouth opened against mine. I felt like I was going to fade away.

She drew back and straightened her dress, fastening the front. "I love you, Jonah," she said softly. "Did you like touching me?"

I nodded.

"I'm glad, because I'm your woman and a man should enjoy feeling his woman."

"Huh?"

"One day I'm going to marry you, Jonah. It's as simple as that. I'm going to be your wife."

"You are?"

"I am."

"Well, now, I—"

"I'm going to make you a good wife! The next time you put your hands all over me like you just did, we're not going to be just playing. It's going to be the real thing. But it'll be all right. We'll be preachered."

Her eyes took on more sparkle. She leaned against me, looking up. "One more thing, Jonah Fletcher. Now that you know what I *look* like naked and what every part of my body *feels* like, you'll have no reason to go exploring with your eyes or hands. If you try, I'll slap you good!"

"You knew I was at the creek watching you?"

"Of course. Do you think I strip naked and preen like a swan for my own pleasure?" She started toward camp.

"You don't know what I look or feel like," I said, not wishing to be outdone by a girl.

She turned, her eyes running over me. She had a little smile on her mouth. "I can wait, Jonah. I can wait." She tilted her head up three notches and marched back to camp.

The day had already been a week long and it wasn't even noon yet. Between her and Sis, a man'd better stay doubly alert!

I ambled toward camp, kicking up clods of grass on the way.

"You looked peaked, Jonah," Sis greeted, looking out from under her old wide-brim.

"I got reason enough," I barked.

"Reckon you do, Jonah," she sassed back. "Reckon you do."

"Jonah peaked?" chimed in Sooey.

"Shut up, Sooey!" I said, but not where it would rile him any.

The redhead smiled. "One thing, Redhead," I snapped. "From now on I'll be the one to do the saying about preening swans, exploring, and feeling!"

"Yes, Jonah."

"And don't you forget it!"

"No, Jonah."

"All right," I said, swinging the Winchester to my shoulder. "Since everybody knows where they stand, move out!"

Sometimes it pays to let womenfolk know who's in charge of things.

In the afternoon, lightning spat as black clouds rolled in. The wind came up, shoving across the slopes. I was more than happy to see the four buildings of the settlement up ahead.

# CHAPTER 5

WE followed the storekeep's directions, finding the Placker place a mile from the settlement. It wasn't what we'd expected. The barn was about to fall down, with some of the boards hanging loose. The house wasn't in much better shape. The door hung crookedly on one hinge. Lack of work showed everywhere.

A man came out onto the porch with a shotgun pointed carelessly in our direction. He wore no shirt, and the sleeves of his red longjohns were rolled. One wide suspender held up his pants. He didn't have a beard—just long whiskers due to neglect.

"Get off my land!"

"Uncle Stu," Jane said quickly. "I'm Jane Placker."

He studied her before lowering the shotgun. "Wal, if you say so. Whatcha doin' here?"

"Pa died. He—he told me to come and stay with you and Aunt Sally."

He grunted. "Sorry about your pa. He was always ailing. Don't surprise me none that he's dead. As for your staying here, we can't feed another mouth."

"Where's Aunt Sally?"

"She works around—down at the Weaver place today. They're readyin' to plant."

"Don't you work this place?" Jane asked.

"That can't be no concern of your'n. I ain't taking in no kin." He was eyeing my Winchester. "That's a fancy rifle, boy. Where'd you get it?"

"It belonged to my pa."

"I've a mind to look at it."

"I reckon not, Mr. Placker."

"I wasn't so much askin' as tellin', boy!"

Pa had a saying: *"We don't push, and by damn, we won't be pushed!"* Funny I should think of that.

"Well, boy?"

"Uncle Stu," Jane pleaded. "He's my friend. You have no reason to ask for his rifle."

"Let the boy answer!"

"I already have."

He wanted to bring the shotgun up. It was in his eyes and the way he shifted his foot. I levered while the rifle rested in the crook of my arm, twisting my body where the barrel pointed just over his right shoulder.

"Better break it open and remove the shells, Placker," Sis said.

He looked from me to her and back to me. He broke the gun open.

"Throw the shells out in the yard," Sis told him.

He pitched them. "You ain't particular what kind of folks you pick for friends, gal," he told Jane.

"Maybe not," she snapped back. "But I prefer their company over yours!" She turned and walked out of the yard. We followed.

We hurried, just making it back to the settlement before the rain broke loose. We ran for the store, making it onto the porch as the flood fell from the sky.

Only Sooey got wet. He had to tie up the mule at the hitching rail. He shoved the horses aside to make room for the mule.

It suddenly turned dark. Lightning cracked everywhere and thunder vibrated against the earth.

Lamps were lit inside and we went in. It was a restaurant, saloon, and general store all in one. It contained about everything a rancher or farmer could need.

We sat at a table near the door. Several ranch hands stood at the bar in back. Most of the tables were near the front, some occupied. One man sat alone on the other side of the room, eating slowly. I thought there was something familiar about him, but his hat was pulled down over his eyes, so I couldn't see his face. The light burned poorly on that side of the room. A rifle lay on the table near his plate.

No one paid us more than a casual glance. Two cowboys came in, their hats and slickers dripping wet. Flashes of lightning lit up the room. During the flashes, we could see through the window out onto the porch, but no farther. It was raining too hard.

The bartender started over to our table. The only hair he had about his head and face was a bushy, white mustache.

"We'd better supper here," Sis said. "We won't be camping out there anytime tonight."

"There's stables out back and a hayloft," said the bartender. "It'll keep you dry. You eating or drinking?"

"Eating," Sis advised.

"Eating," Sooey reaffirmed, chuckling.

The bartender looked him over. "Beans, stew, corn bread, and coffee. It's on the stove in back. Help yourself. You'll find the plates and tools. I'll tally it up when you're through."

He shuffled to the rear. Another man entered the store, looked around and went to the bar.

We filled our plates, poured coffee, and returned to the table. It was comforting to know we had a roof to sleep under later.

But we couldn't decide what to do about Jane. We kept our voices low.

"Jonah." Sis bit off a chunk of corn bread, pointing her fork to the window behind me.

In a flash of lightning, I saw the old man and the dog on the porch, his back to the window.

"I feel cold all of a sudden," Jane said, shivering.

Little tingles began running up my spine.

"The only place I can go is with you, Sis," Jane said.

"Hush. I'm trying to think," Sis said, spooning in some beans.

I felt the tension. Ever since we sat down at the table, I sensed something wrong. It was too quiet. There was a card game at the last table, but the players didn't appear interested. The three at the bar talked in hushed tones. Every man wore a gun belt. A lanky cowboy had been a long time at the door, looking out.

The lone eater across the room was too long at his task. I watched from the corner of my eye as he finally finished, pushing back his plate. He took a sack of Bull Durham from a vest pocket and rolled a smoke. Putting the cigarette to his lips, he made no effort to light it. I still couldn't see his face very good, but I had the feeling he was alert.

I let my right hand move off the table to the Winchester across my lap.

Close thunder shook the building. Lightning popped and cracked out across the prairie. Rain hummed against the roof.

The cowboy standing at the door stepped back as the stocky man entered, everyone immediately aware of his presence. Taking off his yellow slicker, he threw it onto a table. Drops of water fell off his hat as he looked at the man with the unlit cigarette.

A ranch hand brought him a shot of whiskey from the bar. Gulping it down, he wiped a hand over his mouth.

Looking around the room, his penetrating hazel eyes lingered on us. A thick patch of gray hair formed his mustache. The vest was expensive. So were his riding boots. The big pistol on his hip said a lot.

The one who brought him the whiskey remained at his side. They faced the slow eater, their backs more or less to us.

The cardplayers were no longer seated. Those at the bar turned to face the front. Each concentrated on the man seated at the table across the room.

"Seldom see any of your clan traveling alone," the stocky man said at last. There was no hint of anger in his voice. "I'm Carpenter."

"I know who you are, Jim." The seated man didn't even look up. His hands were on the table, fingers entwined.

"Where's the rest of your clan?" Carpenter asked.

"Can't be sure. I've been in the saddle a few days."

"You got nerve, coming back here."

"Just riding through until the storm hit."

"I don't think so."

"Leave it alone, Jim. What's done is done. The past is dead."

"So's my boy."

You'd think they were discussing the storm outside. No one raised his voice or hurried the words. "He was a man and it was his decision."

"He was drinking."

"A lot of men do." He looked up, his clear blue eyes sweeping the room. I figured he was midtwenties. Several days' growth of black whiskers made his tanned, lean face appear hard—which he probably was.

"I'm not looking for trouble, Jim."

"Why are you here anyway?"

"The river's up. Rained a lot out that way. Had no choice but to ride around."

"Too bad. But you must have known what I'd do if you came back here."

"Hadn't thought much about it, Jim. It's not in me to ride a circle for fear someone wants to kill me. A man can't spend his life that way."

"S'pose not," drawled Carpenter. "See your rifle there is already cocked. Strange thing for a man to do."

"Not really."

Two of those at the rear came up to stand near Carpenter, forming a semicircle in front of the table.

"That rifle won't do you any good now," Carpenter was saying.

He came slowly to his feet and moved to one side of the table, jingling a spur. The fingertips of his right hand rested on the table, near the rifle. He wasn't wearing a side arm.

Leather chaps, showing brush scars, covered his long legs. The black shirt and hat made him little more than a dim outline against the wall.

"I take it all these men are backing you, Jim. Am I wrong?"

"Everyone except the trash seated at the table behind me. You could have backed down that day. You could have—"

"Maybe. But we don't push, and by damn—"

"We won't be pushed!" I said, levering as I came to my feet.

The cowboy's hand fell to his gun butt as he whirled around.

"Go ahead," I invited, before I knew what I was saying.

He leveled his eyes from the black barrel of the Winchester to Carpenter, letting his hand fall from his gun.

Carpenter turned halfway around. The lone eater's hands were still on the table but a little closer to the rifle.

Carpenter studied me. "You think you can get us all, boy?" he barked out.

We were in a mess. Every man there was ready. Each gun was under a close, competent hand. My mouth grew dry. I turned the rifle on him, pointing at his middle.

"No. Only going to try for one."

Sis, coming to her feet, pulled her pistol. She held it out with both hands, cocking it. "And me one," she said quietly.

His men waited for a signal. I give them their due. They were a gritty bunch. Carpenter turned back to the table. The man's hand was on the rifle now. He could fire without picking it up.

"Who the hell are they?" Carpenter demanded.

A faint smile touched the other man's mouth. "Kinfolk, I think."

"Damn!" Carpenter said. "Should've known. Where there's one damn Fletcher showing, there's three in the bush!" He looked closely at my rifle. "You and the gal were at Timber Creek, weren't you?"

"We were."

He nodded slowly. "You be Jonah Fletcher?"

"I be him."

He rubbed a palm over his face. He was careful not to let his other hand get close to his gun.

Turning back to the Fletcher at the table, he kept rubbing his face. "What we have here, Fletcher, is a problem."

"*You* have a problem, Jim."

He scratched his chin. The door opened and a tall, slim, large-nosed man in his mid-fifties entered, a rifle in his hand. The black wide-brim sat level on his head. The long black coat and pants were just like the ones Pa always wore. He walked behind me and Sis and toward the bar, his long, stomping stride making his spurs sing just like Pa's always did.

Six tall, rail-slender riflers came through the door after him. One spat tobacco juice on the floor. They passed behind us, stomping long-strided with loud spurs to different parts of the room. Each wore his wide-brim set level, and from under each a pair of blue eyes sized up the situation.

We'd found Uncle Harlan and his bunch of boys—except one. Maybe he was outside. Uncle Harlan flipped the barrel of his rifle over a shoulder. His boys did likewise. The Winchesters were cocked.

"Ka-tri-na," he called in his deep, slow voice. "Come here, baby."

She looked at me, eyes shining. "By damn, Jonah! He sounds just like you."

She ran across the room to him. He lifted her off the floor with his free arm and hugged her good.

The riflers grinned—careful, however, not to be too distracted.

"Who's the redheaded missy?" Uncle Harlan asked, gently moving Sis behind him.

"She's my—" I started. "I mean—"

He lifted his hand. "Missy, you trot on back here."

Jane hurried to the back. He guided her around behind him.

"You armed, Big 'un?" Uncle Harlan directed at Sooey.

"Yethir!" Sooey said, standing up and jerking out his ax. He kicked the table out of the way, sending our supper dishes crashing to the floor. I kept the rifle on Carpenter. His men hadn't moved a muscle since Uncle Harlan pushed through the door.

Uncle Harlan looked over at my slow-eating cousin. "Luke, what passed?"

"Just words, Pa."

He grunted. "It's your move, Jim. You want to leave it at words?"

"There's a rifle cocked at my back. What can I say?"

"Whatever's on your mind."

"Let's leave it at words."

"Uncock, boys," ordered Uncle Harlan.

We all did.

Carpenter and his men left, stepping cautiously around the dog lying on the porch near the door.

I shook hands with my uncle and cousins. Besides Luke, there was Jeremiah, David, Matthew, Simon, and Daniel.

"Where's Solomon?" Sis asked.

"He's back at the ranch," Uncle Harlan said.

I would never be able to tell which was which. They all looked so much alike, each having ample supply of the Fletcher nose and ears. In addition, each spoke the same slow, easy drawl. The youngest was twenty. The oldest twenty-nine.

They shoved tables together and filled plates from the kitchen. We ate a second supper.

I sat beside Jane. Sis was at the end of the table and never stopped asking questions. Right off, she had their names straight. They all had many questions too. They particularly wanted to know the straight of what had happened at Timber Creek.

Sis had a head for details and she told it like it had been.

"Now, you listen," Uncle Harlan said. "Those two you're hunting, Smith and Hollend"— he throwed in some beans, washing it down with steaming coffee—"they're killers of the worst sort. Men don't come no meaner. Whether they operate two small groups or one big one, I don't know. One thing is certain—they pretty well control a section of Kansas north of Abilene."

He gulped more coffee. He didn't offer to help us. That wasn't the Fletcher way. Pa'd told us many times that a Fletcher did his own fighting. Ours was a family matter, left for Sis and me to settle.

What was understood and never needed mentioning was that if you needed help, you sent word to the nearest Fletcher and some sort of help would be forthcoming by the shortcut.

Uncle Harlan and his boys didn't waste much time over a plate. They took out cigars and lit up.

"Now, about this pretty redhead, Jonah," said Uncle Harlan. "She been spoken for properlike?"

"I have." Jane said quickly. "We done made our intentions plain. In time, we'll see a preacher."

Sis put a hand discreetly over her mouth. Uncle Harlan looked up at the ceiling, puffing on his cigar. My cousins did likewise.

"The boy's rather young, missy."

"He's man enough for me!" she shot back, her chin up.

"Katrina," he said, still looking up and puffing. "He's your brother. Does any of this come as a surprise to you?" I had the feeling Uncle Harlan was enjoying himself.

"Jonah knows what he'd be getting."

"I see," he drawled. "Missy, a boy as young as Jonah sometimes changes his mind when he gets older. Mind you, I'm not trying to meddle. Just pointing out how things sometimes work."

"Jonah's free to change his mind whenever he chooses," Jane said. "I don't intend to be his mother. Right now, I'm his woman, and I'll wait for him the rest of my life if he should ask that."

Sis coughed into her hand. Uncle Harlan and his boys were filling up the store with their smoke. "I see," he said. "Appears like you know what you want, missy."

"I know, Mr. Fletcher. I've always known. I've plowed and I've grubbed in the dirt. I planted and I harvested. I've ridden steers and I've slopped and butchered hogs. All the while I dreamed and I waited."

Jeremiah's—or was it Simon's?—cigar was drifting smoke in Jane's face. She reached over and shoved his hand away. "At night, lying in my bed in an old dugout, I dreamed. I ain't ashamed of what I thought about. I wondered what it'd be like with my man."

She didn't even pause for breath. "Well, when I saw Jonah for the first time, I said to myself, 'Jane, that boy ain't just a boy. He's a man and he's your'n!' I said, 'He's the one you've been dreaming about and he's done walked up out of nowhere.' Why, I could tell right off by the way he walked and stood that he wasn't the kind to settle for living in a hole in the ground!"

She looked at me, her green eyes deep as a mountain brook. "He ain't good-looking atall. Fact is, he's on the ugly side until you see what's inside. Well, Mr. Fletcher, I looked deep inside that boy and I saw pretty I didn't know existed!"

"We Fletchers don't run to good looks," Uncle Harlan admitted.

"Well, I can see that," Jane said. "But outside pretty never put food on the table, nohow."

Standing up, she came to his end of the table. "Mr. Fletcher, I've had my say and that's the end of it. If you'll let me stay at your place until Jonah, Sis, and Sooey do what they have to do, I'll be much thankful. I'll wash, cook, and scrub. Hard work is all I know."

"You really decided on him, huh?"

"I've decided," she said, pushing a strand of hair out of her face. "Jonah's mine and he ain't blind to what he'll be getting in return."

Uncle Harlan nodded, standing up. "You'll do just fine, missy. Get ready to ride."

He headed for the bar. "Katrina, will you join me in a little toddy?"

"I'd be proud to, Uncle Harlan."

I went to get Jane's belongings out of the pack. The rain had stopped. Stars appeared in the northern sky. The crisp air smelled fresh.

"I'm going to miss you awful bad, Jonah," she said, patting the mule's forehead.

"I'll be back."

She fussed with my sleeve. "I didn't mean to say you were ugly, Jonah."

"It's the truth, though."

"That's not important, Jonah."

"What you said in there—about knowing the first time you saw me—did you, really?"

"Jonah, I've been waiting for you to come along since I was thirteen! Why, I had you in my mind every night when I lay in my bed and wondered what the future would be like." She touched my nose. "The first time I saw you, I knew, Jonah. I knew."

I cleared my throat.

"Did I embarrass you in there, Jonah?"

I shook my head. Her work-rough hand squeezed mine. For a girl, she had a right firm grip.

Uncle Harlan came out, handing Jane a coat he'd bought in the store. She pulled on her bonnet. My cousins mounted up. One of them took her blanket roll and helped her on the horse behind him. She didn't look back.

Sis looked up at the sky. "We could be up the trail aways by morning," she said.

"We'd best get moving, then," I replied.

Sooey unhitched the mule and we began walking.

"Reckon how many more days before we get to Abilene?"

"We're not going to Abilene. We're going to a place northwest of there. Uncle Harlan said he'd heard Smith and Hollend were at a town called Little Hope."

"That's the name of a town?"

"It is. Luke said if a decent person ever goes there, there's little hope they ever get out alive."

"You're joshing."

"I wish I was, Jonah. I wish I was."

# CHAPTER 6

BEFORE going into Little Hope, we searched the shallow glen for a likely place to camp, finding a good spot about a mile or so from town. Sooey cleaned out a sleeping area under an oak while I gathered stones from the stream bed to build a suitable ring for our fire.

Toward late afternoon, we walked to town. Of the five saloons, only two appeared to have many customers. A boardwalk ran the length of the row of buildings on each side of the wide, wagon-rutted street. Most of the structures were board. The bank, crowded between a café and a harness shop, had a stone front. The assorted sizes of the false fronts bespoke the carpenter's stiff resistance to conformity.

I didn't think it was a good place to build. You walked up a rise toward the center of the town regardless of which end of the street you entered. And, since one side of the street was on higher ground than the other, one was constantly stepping down or up. You couldn't go anywhere without tripping on steps.

We stopped in front of the marshal's office—partly because he was sitting out on the walk, but mostly because we were curious how a one-legged man with a black patch over his right eye ever got to be town marshal in the first place.

"Nice town," I said.

His good eye examined the Winchester on my shoulder. He must have been in his late thirties. His thin shoulders leaned forward. The star, pinned to a faded blue shirt, showed tarnish. He looked up and down the street. Crudely built crutches lay on the boardwalk beside his chair.

"Little Hope used to be," he said, an emptiness in his voice.

"It's more a state of mind now. You folks just come in?"

I nodded.

"Better complete your business and move on." He searched the street again, his long, narrow face expressionless. The mustache seemed to give substance where there was none.

"You running us out of town?" Sis inquired sharply.

"With what? This empty gun strapped to my bad side? I'm a joke, miss. It's their way of letting the folks hereabout know they run this county!"

"Who's they?" I asked.

A woman at the saloon across the street screamed. Laughter and curses followed. Those along the street ignored it.

"'They' means Oates Smith, Marvin Hollend, and the filth who work for them. All killers and rapists trying to act like businessmen."

"They made you marshal?" I prodded.

"The town council did. About a year ago. After the real marshal vanished."

He saw Sooey staring at the nub that used to be a leg. "Lost it at Vicksburg," he seemed anxious to explain. "My eye, too. Was with Grant's army when he took Mississippi."

There'd been a hint of pride in his voice for a moment. He waited until the wagon passed. "Now, best you move on." He hunted the street again. "You stay and you'll likely end up in the mine."

"By damn, we will!"

"Oh, not you, miss. Just the big one and the boy. You'd be put to work up there." He nodded toward a large two-story house on the knoll overlooking the town. "That's where the council assigns young girls."

"What's up there?" Sis's curiosity was up.

He gave the street another survey. "A brothel."

Four ranch hands rode in. "Howdy, Marshal," One of them said as they neared.

Another added an insulting obscenity and they all laughed. The marshal's face took on a tinge, but he didn't say anything.

"Maybe you should load that six-shooter," I surmised.

His brownish eye leveled at me. "What can half a man do?" he snapped.

I didn't answer. He didn't need me to remind him that you don't need two legs to pull a trigger.

"Look, boy!" He must have guessed what I was thinking. "Smith and Hollend came in here over a year ago with a bunch of armed men and took this county. Those who protested or tried to fight were either found dead or not found at all. A few were even tied to a wagon wheel out there in the street and got their backs shredded by Smith's bullwhip!"

The eye flared. "Be damn slow to judge when you don't know the price! Sure, I protested. The council assigned my wife to that house up yonder and me to be the town clown." He looked down at his one leg. "She was one of the brave ones. She killed herself."

"Where can we find Smith and Hollend?" Sis asked.

Wiping his eye, his voice returned to its empty hopeless sound. "They took over the Townsend place—the Lazy T. It's north of here aways. Covers most of the county. Those four bastards who just rode in ride for the brand. When Hollend ain't in town, he's likely out there."

"And Smith?" Sis said.

"The Whip?" He spat in the street. "You can find him whipping the men at the coal mine or whipping the women up yonder."

More riders approached. The marshal pulled his hat lower and leaned forward, looking at the walk. That was one way to avoid insults. The men rode by without a word.

Three two-horse wagons rumbled in, their wheels protesting against the ruts. Stopping near the center of town, men, their faces smudged with coal dust, climbed out of the wagons, some making for the saloons. Others dispersed to the small houses and shanties scattered about behind the town buildings.

Several women, mostly young ones, came from various places and climbed into the first wagon. The driver turned around in the street, heading for the house on the knoll. The sun was just going down.

"Assignees," the marshal said. "A sundown-to-sunup job. They get to keep a third of what they earn."

As the wagon squeaked past, one of the girls looked at me. She could not have been more than fourteen.

"That's how the council works," said the marshal, matter of fact.

"What in hell is the council?" Sis demanded.

"A group of the town's so-called leading citizens appointed by Smith and Hollend," he advised. "Men who want to continue living. The banker, a saloon owner. A few others. They claim they have no choice about what they do."

He laughed. It sounded as empty as his voice. "But, I've noticed they started making assignments with zeal since Hollend started paying them a bonus for each man or woman they assign."

For the first time I noticed the larger saloon had SMITH AND HOLLEND printed in bold letters on the false front. Several of the other business establishments had similar letters.

The marshal picked up his crutches and stood up. "Take my advice. Leave." He looked at my rifle again. "That's a heavy piece for a boy."

"It does tire me sometimes," I admitted.

He went into the office. Sis turned, tugging at her pants. "By damn! We got them now, Jonah!"

"We have?"

"Thure," assured Sooey.

We moved down the street. I stopped. The old man was tying his horse to the hitching rail in front of the Smith and Hollend Saloon, which, we later learned, was referred to as the S and H. He climbed the steps and limped across the porch, carrying the long double-barrel inside.

The dog growled his way under the porch and pawed up the dirt, digging a cool hole.

"Maybe the old man works for Smith and Hollend," Sis speculated.

"That would explain a lot of things," I said.

"Keep your voice down," Sis cautioned.

Several on the walk paused to look at us. Sooey put his hand under his blanket-wrap, close to his ax.

Sis wasn't satisfied with a trek up and down the street. She had to poke into every nook and corner. We found our way behind the buildings and even looked around in the livery stable—a long, low barn whose loft was filled with hay and sacks of grain. I was glad it was dark. Otherwise, we might have caused suspicion.

We peeked into all the saloons and several of the stores. At the S and H Saloon, we took a look inside through a small window from the alley.

The smoke-filled room was crowded. Women, their fronts almost as bare as their shoulders, moved among the customers, laughing and joking. The old man sat alone at a table sipping a beer. The shotgun was across his lap. When he finished the beer, a young blond woman came up behind him. Leaning over, she whispered in his ear. Light from the lamps hanging overhead cast a pleasant glow down the low-cut red dress and over her swelling breasts. She ran fingers through her short hair and the curls bounced right back. I thought she was real pretty and I said as much.

"Jonah!" scolded Sis.

The blond moved slowly through the crowd and climbed the stairs to the second floor, entering one of the tiny rooms off the balcony. After a few minutes, the old man left the table and went upstairs.

"Appears he's been here before," Sis said.

"Seems like."

Down the street, near the end of town, a six-shooter blasted the night. Two men on horseback galloped along the street, waving their hats and yelling. Somewhere, a guitar player strummed a few chords.

At another saloon, two men fought each other through the door and out into the street. A few gathered around, urging more blows and eye-gouging.

"They're not in town," Sis said quietly.

She was the only one who would recognize Smith and Hollend, since she had seen them commit their foul crime. Their ugly faces were etched in her memory forever.

No, she would never forget what they looked like. Now I wanted to see their faces too. I wanted to see their eyes over the sights of the Winchester as I pulled the trigger and made them pay for what they done to Pa and Hester.

Sis leaned against the building. Sooey adjusted his ax and joined her.

"They murdered, stole, and raped their way across Texas, and now they have this town in their grasp, still raping, stealing, and killing!" said Sis through gritted teeth.

"But not for long," I reassured her.

"That's right, Jonah. Not for long."

We left the alley, keeping to the shadows in the middle of the street as we headed out of town toward camp.

"I'm hungry, Thister," Sooey complained.

"I am, too, Sooey," Sis said. "And I do believe there's a can of peaches left."

Sooey chuckled, picking up his pace. We practically had to run to keep up with him.

When Sooey had the fire going, he removed his blanket-wrap, pulled out his ax, and went to work on the large, uprooted oak nearby. The chips flew as the ax dug deep in rapid blows.

"What's he doing, Jonah?"

I shrugged.

Chips continued to fly in large chunks as Sooey warmed up. I figured he was just going through one of his spells of wanting to do something spectacular to impress Sis. It was during such a spell in Texas that he picked up a pony Sis thought was cute and brought it to her.

By the time supper was ready, he'd hefted two big logs in and threw them down. He arranged them side by side, stood back to survey his handiwork, and then rolled one log about six feet from the other. He sat down on one of them, wiping the sweat off his forehead with his blanket-wrap.

"Make good theats," he said.

"We didn't need two logs for seats," I said, perching beside him.

A big finger jabbed at the space between the logs. "If we fight, you and Thister can thoot from behind log," he said, picking his words slowly. "Like a . . . a barricade."

Times like this proved that Sooey wasn't stupid. Sis handed him a heaping plate of beans, hoecake, and sowbelly.

"Good thinking, Sooey," she said.

He chuckled, taking a deep breath and looking around for another big tree to cut up.

The mule's head came up, ears alert. I levered the Winchester, dropping down behind the barricade. Sis and Sooey moved away from the fire, into the dark.

The rider pulled up, dismounting away from the light of the fire. "Hello," a woman called softly, walking into the light. It was the blond in the low-cut red dress.

"You alone?" I asked.

"Yes."

I didn't trust her. "What do you want?"

"The old man with the dog sent me."

I uncocked the rifle and stood up. If the old man had wanted us dead, he would have killed us a long time ago—or sent Sweetie to do it for him.

"Could I please have a cup of that coffee?" she said, sitting on the log near me. She wasn't any older than Sis.

She tasted the coffee. "You'll need horses."

"We're used to walking," I replied.

She ignored the remark. "Go to the livery stable tomorrow, after dark. There'll be three horses in the end stalls. They'll be saddled. Leave your mule in the corral behind the livery."

"Why?" Sis wanted to know. "Why is the old man being so generous?"

"It doesn't matter," she said. "You don't have to take the horses if you don't want."

"Who are you?" Sis asked, removing her wide-brim.

"My name is Henrietta. Everyone calls me Henry."

"Well, Henry, we're not sure the old man can be trusted any more than we can be sure about you," Sis advised.

"He said you would be cautious." She handed me her cup, ran a hand down inside the dress, and withdrew a folded envelope. From it, she removed a key.

"This fits the back door to the Dry Goods store," she told us, handing the key to Sis. "He said to tell you that everything you might need is there; that you should never use the key until after dark when the town has quieted down."

Sis studied the key. "Who is he, Henry?"

"I can't say. I don't really know." She looked quickly at each of us. "He's very strange and that's a most vicious dog he has." She stood up. "He said that death had come to Little Hope riding the three winds."

"That old man is crazy," Sis said.

"Is he? That's the name of the horses in the three stalls."

"Each horse is named Wind?" I said.

She nodded. "Yes. Isn't that strange?"

I sure thought so.

"I guess that makes us 'death,'" Sis said, only half-joking.

"I have to go now," said Henry, giving Sis a strange look. "If I'm away too long, they'll miss me. Smith gave one girl ten lashes for leaving without permission."

"His whipping days are drawing to a close," said Sis.

Henry looked at each of us. "Yes. Death has come riding the three Winds."

When she'd ridden out, Sis looked at me. "Jonah, you suppose everyone in this town is a lunatic?"

I shrugged. "If Henry is, she's a pretty one. That dress reveals of lot of—"

"Jonah!"

"I wasn't going to say what you're thinking."

She jerked her hat on. "Once a boy has seen what came from a rib, he's never the same again."

"I think I'll eat," I told her.

We took our plates and sat on the log. It was Sooey's third helping. Beyond the camp, night sounds reminded me of home. The Kansas wind caressed the tree branches, rustling the leaves. Sooey threw a stick on the coals. Sparks drifted away.

"You think much about Jane?" Sis asked.

"Some."

"She's got ways."

"She has."

"Never saw a girl so sure of what she wanted and how to get it," she allowed.

I sipped my coffee.

"By damn, Jonah! I could learn a thing or two from her."

I sipped again.

"Which is better?" she asked after a while. "The looking or the feeling?"

"Huh?"

She swallowed some coffee. "I'm not prying. I'd just like to know, that's all."

"You mean if I had my druthers?"

"Yes."

"Both."

"Jo-nah!"

I fetched the pot and poured us another cup. Sis straddled the log, facing me. Sooey threw on another stick and bit off a chew. He was drowning belly worms again.

"One thing's for sure, Jonah. With her under your blanket, you'd not have to worry about frostbite," she reckoned, a grin forming on her mouth.

The coffee was hot. I swallowed anyway. "You got a plan worked out yet?"

"No, but I'm giving it some thought. They did the same thing here as Soltz did at Timber Creek; built their own little kingdom on the fears of others, killing and taking—forcing folks to bow to their every little whim."

"That's what Soltz did, alright."

"We do the same thing here as we did there. We take them down piece by piece, get rid of everything that's important to them, and when there's nothing left, we make our settlement."

"And how do you figure we're going to do all that?"

"I don't know, Jonah. But we will."

"I'd just as soon shoot them right off and leave this place."

"I want them to pay for what they did. Just killing them is not enough!"

"All right. What's first?"

"We're going to burn that whorehouse down."

I thought on it. "Might as well."

# CHAPTER 7

THE large shining black stallions eyed us suspiciously. We led them out at the rear of the livery. They snorted and nickered, heads high and nostrils flaring.

We took a while admiring them as they pranced and stomped the ground.

"Let's see if they can run," Sis said as I slid my rifle into the scabbard.

We hardly had time to sit saddle. They lunged, seeming to gain full stride in the first leap, each fighting to get ahead of the other. We had to hold onto our hats.

The ground at their feet was a blur as we rode across the prairie, making a wide circle. It was almost like sitting in a rocking chair, their motion being so smooth.

We watered them at a stream. I don't think the three Winds wanted to stop. When we dismounted, they pawed at the ground with impatience.

"Horses aren't suppose to run that fast," Sis said admiringly, patting hers on the neck.

"These do."

"These are not horses, Jonah. They're the wind."

Sooey hugged his horse around the neck. The stallion did not seem to mind.

"Wonder where the old man got them?" I wondered aloud.

"Who knows?" Sis answered. "I quit trying to put sense in what he does."

We mounted and held on. If you weren't quick, they'd leap clear out from under you. In no time, we were back at the livery. Henry was waiting for us. She looked much better in a regular dress. The blue muslin fit close, attracting my eye right away.

The mule was gone. I asked her about it.

"The old man had someone hitch her to a wagon and drive out to the abandoned fort. He said you were camped too close to town, that it was too dangerous."

She gave us directions to the fort. "There's supplies in the wagon. . . . Please be careful."

The fort was ten miles from town. The upright logs of the outer stockade leaned over in places. Most of the small buildings were in one form of dilapidation or another. Several of the roofs were caved in. Part of the covering of the stables still stood, however.

The small log building with the barred windows and heavy wooden door seemed solid enough to shed rain and bullets.

The mule, unhitched and eating grain in a stall, appeared contented. The wagon was under a section of good roof. It contained all sorts of supplies.

"I have questions for that old man," Sis said.

"You won't get any answers."

We looked around. The fort, on high ground, overlooked a lazy, shifting expanse of grass.

We unsaddled the horses and fed them grain sent out with the wagon. Sooey found a spring at the cluster of trees below the rear of the fort and filled up the water barrel attached to the side of the wagon. I searched through the buildings.

It wasn't long before I smelled frying salt pork, flapjacks, and beans. Sooey found a case of canned peaches in the wagon and decided it was time he had a whole can to himself.

After sundown, we saddled the horses. It was all we could do to hold them to a trot. Once a foot hit a stirrup, the three Winds forgot how to walk.

We entered the town after midnight, going in from the back. A few people were still about, and three saloons and the cafe were still open. The key fit and I pushed open the rear door slowly. Sis found the coal oil and we each took a can.

I snapped the heavy padlock closed and we led the stallions silently away, working our way around the low hill.

At the bottom of the knoll, we entered a washout. The gulley was deep and we moved along in single file.

Lights showed through the many windows of the brothel. A piano player switched to something slow. Several buggies were tied up at the back. Horses dozed at the various hitching rails.

A man came out onto the back porch, stepped to the edge, and unbuttoned his fly. When he was through, he staggered back inside.

At one of the upstairs windows, a woman moved in front of the curtainless window. She had nothing on. A man, equally bare, came up behind her and they caressed and fondled. After a minute or two, they moved away from the window.

We sat down, leaning against the side of the gulley. Sooey held the reins as he chewed.

It was a long wait. At sunup, they began clearing out. The wagon drove up in the front and the whores and young assignees climbed aboard.

We waited another hour, hoping whoever owned the fancy buggy in back and the saddle horse at the side would leave.

"We can't wait all day," Sis advised. She adjusted her hat, making certain all hair was tucked under. "You keep the rifle ready."

I followed her up out of the gulley. Sooey stayed with the horses.

She carried two cans of oil. I took the third and the Winchester.

The only way to approach the house was as if you were on an innocent errand. Approaching the back porch, however, we decided to kneel down and listen.

Hearing nothing, we proceeded up the steps and inside, entering a wide hall. The kitchen door stood open and we quietly entered the hot room. In the parlor, a man and woman argued.

"I don't give a damn what you say!" the woman spoke in a grating, husky voice. "We need more girls—young ones."

"There aren't any more," the man snapped.

"There are plenty in the surrounding counties!"

"Don't be stupid. An operation like this has to stay local, where you can control the townspeople. We start taking girls from those places and the whole damn state will come down on us."

A chair raked across the floor. "Let's get some coffee," she said.

We made a dash for the pantry. I pulled the door almost closed. Sis breathed heavily against the back of my neck.

Entering the kitchen, the heavy-set woman poured the coffee. Thick rouge covered her flat face. Thin lips left a pink smudge on the rim of the cup. They sat at the table, her breasts nearly spilling out over the yellow dress onto the table.

The man gulped his coffee. Tiny red stripes separated the rich blue of his suit. The white collarless shirt lay open at the neck, revealing a heavy mat of black hair. Small, dark eyes stared at the woman from under the gray Stetson. His silver-plated Colt fit neatly into a cut-down holster. Slowly, he smiled, his crooked mouth seeming to resist the effort.

"I'd double the profits," the woman said.

"Then hire more whores."

"They don't want wore-out tramps! They want the young, pretty stuff."

"There ain't any left."

"Have your men scout the farms and ranches," she insisted. "There must be two or three girls they missed."

"Awright! But no one under fifteen."

"Fourteen," she argued. "Hell, I'll let you break them in."

He laughed—a high-pitched sound. Sis dug fingers into my arm.

"Think about it," she encouraged. "Young ones. Little heifers with handful-size breasts and firm behinds—ready to bull. They'd bring top dollars."

He wet his lips. "Tessie, the council won't like it," he warned. "They said no less than fifteen years old."

"Yeah, but we got them to come down before, didn't we?

They'll come around, you'll see." She laughed. "Hell, you ain't afraid of them, are you?"

His face flushed into a scowl. Long, slim fingers tapped the gun butt. "I'm afraid of no man. Don't you ever hint that I am!"

Tessie put down her cup. "Get me the girls. Soon as you bull them good," she tittered, "I'll put them to work."

He came out of his trance. "You going back to town?"

"No. Think I'll catch a nap first. It's been a long night." She went down the hall and upstairs.

Soon we heard him ride off. We stepped out of the pantry.

Sis was white. "That was Hollend, Jonah," she whispered.

"What do we do? The woman's upstairs."

"What we came to do." She poured a can of oil along the kitchen wall.

"What about her?"

*"Ssshhh!"*

She picked up another can and went into the parlor and quickly poured oil on a rug along a wall.

"Sis?"

The last can she poured on the furniture and walls of the large room with the piano. Then, going to the bottom of the stairs, she pounded the wall with the butt of her six-shooter.

"What the hell is it?" Tessie screamed down from her room.

"The house is on fire!" Sis yelled.

A door jerked open. "What?"

"The house is on fire," Sis repeated.

"I don't smell smoke."

"You'd better get out of here, you old hussy, if you don't want to burn!" Sis called back. She struck a match and threw it to the rug on the parlor floor. I set fire in the big room. After Tessie ran screaming out the door in her underwear, we fired the hall and kitchen.

Down the hill toward the gulley we ran, hearing Tessie yelling as she scurried toward town.

I was out of breath when we reached the horses. At the

house, black smoke poured out the windows. "We'd best ride," Sis said, swinging into the saddle.

We rode south. At a rivulet, we urged our horses in and turned downstream to cover our tracks. Near the road leading to the mine, Sis turned west and we let the horses stretch out for a while.

Later, we swung in the direction of the abandoned fort. The three Winds were still anxious and we let them have their way. Off in the distance, heavy smoke curled skyward.

It was cool at the spring below the fort where we paused to let the horses drink their fill. Later, while Sooey and I unsaddled and rubbed down the animals, Sis set about fixing a meal.

The next night, we left Sooey and the stallions at the corral behind the livery. At the other end of town, a noisy crowd gathered. Torches lit up the street.

The marshal sat in front of his office. Sis and I crossed the street. He saw us and reached for his crutches. Something changed his mind. He let them drop.

"You still here?"

"You see us, don't you?" Sis said.

He took off his battered hat, wiping a soiled red handkerchief across his forehead. Replacing the hat, he looked toward the crowd. "They'll kill her," he mumbled.

"Who?" Sis asked.

"One of the assignees to the brothel. Tessie said a woman set the fire, and she thinks it was the Logan girl." His eye held on Sis. "They're going to use the whip on her. Seems she's been giving them a lot of trouble lately."

"Who's going to use the whip on her?" Sis asked quickly.

"Tonight, Smith is letting his second-in-command do the honors."

Sis pulled me around behind the jail. "Go get Sooey and the horses," she said, breathless. "Meet me behind the Dry Goods. Hurry!"

I ran to the livery. Sooey followed me to the Dry Goods, leading the horses. Sis came out of the store carrying two cans of coal oil. Quickly, she snapped the padlock.

I followed her behind the buildings. The crowd seemed louder. Shadows made by the torches danced through the alley and against the shanties.

The last building on our side of the street was a Smith and Hollend warehouse of some sort. We quietly made our way behind it. Sis tried the rear door. It was locked.

"Sooey!" she called.

Handing me the reins, he hastened up the steps. Under Sis's instructions, he put a shoulder against the door and shoved. It splintered open.

Inside, Sis poured the two cans of oil on a pile of empty burlap sacks.

"Hey!" came the demand from the corner. "Whatcha doing there?"

I moved back against the building, fading into the darkness.

"I said whatcha doing in there?"

As he brushed past, I swung the barrel of the Winchester against the back of his head. He thumped to the ground.

Out front, yells went up.

Sis rushed down the steps. She handed Sooey several matches. "When you hear Jonah shoot, you set fire to the oil, understand?"

"I will, Thister."

"As soon as you set the fire, mount up." She pointed toward a group of shanties. "Head that way. We'll catch up."

He nodded. "I set fire when Jonah thoots. I ride that way—"

Yells from the street drowned out the rest of his words. I moved around the side of the building. Sis led our two Winds.

I couldn't see over the crowd. "Maybe I can see from the saddle," I whispered to her.

"The horse won't stand still, Jonah!"

I mounted anyway, holding the reins tightly. I felt the stallion's body quiver under me, his muscles stiffening, ready to lunge. I held the reins tighter and nudged with my knees. He stomped forward to the corner. I held my breath, hoping he wouldn't leap out.

"Lay it on, Leech!" a man called from the circle to the small, thin man with the whip. "Make her tell the truth."

Her arms spread, her hands tied to the rear wagon wheel, she faced them on her knees, her back against the wheel hub.

Leech went up to her, saying something. She screamed an oath at him. Laughing, he grabbed the front of her dress and began ripping and tearing, baring her to the waist. A few yelled deliriously.

No one moved to help her. Several armed townspeople stood motionless, watching. A few even shouted encouragement to Leech. A few women, mingled in the circle of onlookers, watched silently.

Leech paced off the distance, turned to face the girl, and uncoiled the whip. He popped the tip near her knees. She flinched, ducking her head down. She was the young girl I'd seen in the wagon on our first day in town.

Planting his feet for the swing, Leech looked over at the short, stout man in the light brown suit. The round face broke into a thin smile as he nodded. He had to be Oates Smith, and I would have shot the son of a bitch in the belly if Sis had not been there.

Someone yelled as Leech went into motion. I put the first bullet through his belt. The stallion flinched. I held the reins tightly in my teeth, holding him steady.

Levering, I put the second bullet above the tag of the tobacco sack hanging out of his left vest pocket. He jerked around, bellowing.

A gun belched fire from the fringe of the crowd. It was too late. The stallion stretched out, hooves reaching for distance. Flames leaped out at the back of the warehouse.

Up ahead, Sooey darted past the shanties. Shouts and curses rose from the town as people rushed for water buckets and horses.

Sooey waited for us near the crest of a swell. Swinging down, I handed Sis the reins and adjusted the rear sight.

Going to my right knee, I waited, rifle steady. Men on horses gathered near the burning building, hollering orders at one another. When they started our way, I began firing, emptying the rifle. One man yelped as the .44 kicked him out of the saddle. Two horses went down. The others made their way out of the confusion and came on.

I hit the saddle. The fort was north, but we turned westward. I took shells from my pocket and reloaded.

"Now we race!" Sis yelled in the ears of her horse.

She was almost jerked out of the saddle. The moon was out now and the night wind cool. Sis snatched off her hat, holding it in her free hand. Her hair caught the wind as she leaned forward.

She led, with Sooey and me following close behind. We didn't push the horses. There was no need. Running was in their blood. Soon they settled down, breathing hard as their sure-footed hooves pounded in rhythm.

I kept searching the prairie behind us. Only once did I see our pursuers, tiny black specks against the moonlit horizon.

We slowed the horses some, but they would not tolerate much of that nonsense. Later, when we dismounted at water, we listened, our ears to the ground. There was nothing. After a brief rest, the stallions became anxious to leave. We headed for the fort.

At sunup, we reached camp. Henry had coffee boiling. Sweetie, crouching near her, offered his usual greeting.

# CHAPTER 8

"SHUT up!" Henry yelled at Sweetie. "You growled all the way out here and I'll not listen to any more of it." She shook a stick of firewood at him.

He quieted. However, when I looked at him, he curled his lips in distasteful silence. He was careful not to disturb Henry.

She wore a riding skirt, boots, and a red flannel shirt. She poured our tin cups full and we sat on the ground around the fire. From the corner of my eye, I saw her casting a look my way.

"You're young, and yet you're not." Her voice was soft.

"Why are you here?" Sis asked.

"The old man wants you to be prepared to move your camp."

"By damn, we're not gypsies!"

"He said you should keep moving around; if they located your camp, they'd likely set up a trap or ambush."

"We keep a watch," I said.

She studied me. "There's an old homestead eight miles east of here," she continued. "No one lives there. If you need to move, you'll find supplies already there. The soddy is partially hidden among trees near a creek." She went on to tell how to find the place.

"If we decide to move, we'll take a look," Sis said. "I don't think anyone could tell who we were last night, though."

"If they did, I haven't heard about it," Henry replied. "Nothing but confusion abounds in Little Hope right now. The warehouse burned to the ground, by the way."

She turned to me. "And you're so young for such as this."

"Close to sixteen," I said.

"He's fifteen," corrected Sis.

Henry looked at me over the rim of her cup. "Looks more like seventeen."

I sat up straighter.

Draining her cup, Henry stood up. "I must be going." She climbed into the saddle. "Come on, dog. You can growl all the way back."

"I'm beginning to like that girl," Sis said, watching her ride out.

"I like her too," Sooey put in.

"She is fetching," I admitted.

Sis cast a glance at me. "We'd better eat and get some sleep. We've a lot to do tonight."

At sundown we saddled up. We took the mule and pack to bring back the dynamite.

While Sis and I looked about, Sooey stayed with the horses and the mule at the rear of the livery. The saloons were noisy, even the smaller ones. Since the brothel fire, the professionals worked out of the shanties and the tiny rooms on the second floor of the two larger saloons. A couple of the women were less particular, using the livery loft. They probably didn't have to split the money they earned on the hay.

The girl assignees were temporarily free. Tessie, according to the marshal, was pressuring the council to let the assignees use the church building until the house on the knoll could be rebuilt.

We sat on the steps to the jail. The marshal occupied the chair on the walk.

"No one knows who set the fires or shot Leech," the marshal said, prodding. "'Course, if I know'd, I wouldn't let on. It's time someone fought back."

I polished the barrel of the Winchester with the sleeve of my coat. "They didn't catch the shooter?"

"Lost the trail out yonder," he replied, his eye holding me. "Had to be at least two of them, I figure."

We said nothing.

A portly pedestrian crossed the street, coming toward us. He walked up to Sis, standing over her, his hands thrust in his front pockets. A heavy gold chain hung across the front of his vest.

"Where are you people assigned?" he demanded in an authoritative manner.

"That's the banker," the marshal advised. "He's head of the council."

"Shut up!" he ordered the marshal. "Answer me!" he yelled at us. He stood straight, his double chin in a neat fold.

"We don't take assignments," Sis advised, sounding reasonably pleasant.

"See here, girl!"

Sis shoved the Colt up against his belly.

"I'm—I'm not armed!" he sputtered.

"That's too bad, mister." She cocked the pistol.

"Marshal?"

"Don't call on me. I ain't allowed to load my pistol." He spat in the street.

Sis stood, staring up into the banker's face. "If you or your council ever assign or even think about assigning another girl to whoredom, we'll do some assigning ourselves!"

"I think she means six feet down," the marshal explained gleefully.

"Smith nor Hollend won't—"

"Shut your mouth!" Sis advised abruptly, "and get your fat belly from in front of my pistol!"

He ran, stumbling down the street. Sis holstered. "By damn, Jonah! I came close to shooting him."

The marshal chuckled. "Don't reckon he'll be telling anyone about that little incident. But whoever is out there raising this ruckus had better be on guard—not only against Smith and Hollend but also against the townspeople. Most will side with them bastards, and they can be vicious."

He picked up his crutches. "There were more locals than gang members riding out last night for Leech's killer."

"Where's the Logan girl now?" Sis asked.

"Tessie took her out to the Lazy T this afternoon."

"Why?"

"I don't know and I don't want to know," he returned bluntly.

"Jonah?"

We rushed up the street and down the alley. We had to wait for the man and woman in the back of the wagon parked near the store to finish their arguing and lovemaking. They carried on both activities simultaneously.

"Slut," Sis decided.

From the Dry Goods, we loaded a case of dynamite, caps, and fuses on the mule. Covering it up with the canvas, we mounted up.

In the southwest, a storm was brewing. Distant lightning outlined the dark clouds. Sis gave Sooey his instructions, telling him to lead the mule back to the fort and wait there.

"I'll be careful, Thister," he said, leading the mule off.

The stallions wanted to run. We let them. Their steel-shod hooves pounded the earth as we gained the prairie.

The large ranch house and outbuildings sat in the middle of a long, narrow stretch of level land. A creek flowed among the trees behind the barns, making its way down the shallow valley. The ground swelled gradually to where we dismounted, overlooking the place.

Lamps burned in several of the rooms at the house. The bunkhouse, a long, low building down near one of the barns, issued light from several small windows. The door opened and a man walked out, going to a shack nearby, where a lamp glowed dimly.

He was inside for a half hour. When he returned to the bunkhouse, another left, hurrying to the shack. Both men wore only underwear bottoms.

When a third visited the shack, Sis stood up. "I think we found her, Jonah."

"That's Hollend's headquarters, Sis."

She mounted. "Coming?"

I climbed into the saddle. Swinging out, we headed toward the trees down behind the shack. A horse in the corral whinnied. The stallions did not reply.

Tying the reins to a limb, we crossed the opening, crouched and running. We reached the safety of the dark at the rear of the shack.

"Please . . . not again . . . oh please," a girl inside pleaded.

"Shut up, bitch!" A fist hit flesh.

We moved around to the side. No one was about. The girl begged again and was answered with a curse and a slap.

I pushed open the door slowly. Thick, dark hair covered the man's wide, heavy shoulders. He spread himself over her, grabbing the thin, naked body into his huge arms. She tried to protest again, but the sudden weight of him stifled the words.

She moaned. I swung the rifle, the barrel crashing against the side of his head. He grunted mournfully, eyes rolling back. I slammed the barrel into his face, knocking him off her.

She started to scream. Sis clamped a hand over her mouth, speaking softly all the while.

The rapist lay moaning on the floor, his expansive frame jerking. I levered, pointing the muzzle against his temple.

*"Jonah!"*

"I'll kill him!"

"You pull that trigger and we'll never get out of here alive!"

She pulled a blanket around the girl. I cracked open the door. The way was clear. We scurried out and behind the shack. At the house, someone ran out of the root cellar, threw down a basket, and rushed inside.

"Hurry up, Brutus! It's my turn with her!" came a holler from the bunkhouse.

We made a dash for the horses, helping the Logan girl along between us.

Sis hit the saddle. I helped the girl up behind her. "Meet you at the top of the hill," I said.

"What are you going to do, Jonah?"

"Get going and keep it quiet."

I led the stallion down the creek through the trees. Tying him to a bush, I ran, bent over, toward the big barn.

"Brutus! Hurry it up, dammit!"

I struck a match to the hay piled against a wall and dashed out. I was in the saddle when the alarm sounded.

*"Fire!"*

The stallion quivered with anticipation. I held him to a fast walk until we left the trees. He bounded up the swell in a fit of aggravation.

I dismounted. Sis took the reins. The girl was gasping in silent sobs. She was beat up pretty bad.

Slipping the rear sight, I stretched out on the ground and waited. Men, casting long, distorted shadows, ran with buckets.

I saw one of the rapists. He carried two buckets, almost losing his bottoms. Keeping him fined to the sights, I let my finger squeeze the trigger.

The crack of the rifle echoed above the yells below, reverberating against the up-and-down landscape.

Whether he fell or not, I did not know. While he was screaming, I searched for the other one.

He turned to look in my direction, dropping the bucket. I aimed for his middle, just above the band of his bottoms.

He jerked double when the bullet hit, turning over the bucket of water as he fell.

They scattered out of the light, away from the barn. Tessie appeared in the doorway of the house, silhouetted by the light from inside.

I fired. In my haste, I yanked on the trigger. She slammed the door shut just as the frame splintered.

I unloaded the rifle into the lighted windows as men scrambled for horses at the corral. I carefully reloaded.

"Will you hurry, Jonah?" Sis handed me the reins.

By first light, we'd circled far out from the fort and stopped at water to let the horses drink and rest. Sis helped the girl down and over to sit under a tree. I kept my eyes running from crest to crest, knowing the pursuers were probably far behind even if they'd managed to pick up our trail.

When Sis came up behind me, and when she spoke, her voice was empty. "She's dead, Jonah."

# CHAPTER 9

THE next two days passed slowly. Sis said little, keeping to herself, currying her stallion or moping down at the spring. I wondered how long it would be before the gang came down on us.

Finally, she decided it was time to get back to work. I carried the sticks of dynamite in my coat pockets. She carried the caps and fuses. The three of us moved out after dark.

As we approached the Lazy T ranch house, we rode around the herd of cattle milling at the beginning of the valley.

Dismounting on the back side of the incline, we walked to the top and lay down, watching the activity below. A half moon hid behind a thin patch of clouds. Several men with rifles loitered near the porch.

The fire had destroyed the barn. A fringe-top buggy pulled up in front of the house with two men on horseback following. They, too, carried rifles. When Hollend came out and climbed into the buggy, they headed toward town.

"They must be expecting trouble," Sis said, smiling for the first time in two days. She sat up. "How are we going to blow up the house with all those guards around, Jonah?"

I shrugged. "Looks like we can't."

"We'll find a way."

"How?"

"I'm thinking about it!"

Sooey tried to help her think, chewing his tobacco thoughtfully.

"We could throw a few shots down there," I suggested. "Maybe they'd all come after us and we could work back and set the dynamite."

"And maybe the guards would stay put, too."

"Well, you think of something then." I lay on my back, head resting in my hands, looking at the sky. A big cloud chased the smaller ones from under the moon. The breeze disturbed the grass along the swell. I nearly dozed.

"Jonah!"

I jumped up, rifle in hand.

"We can do it!"

"Huh?"

She stood up, pulling at her pants and adjusting the gun belt.

I looked to where she pointed. "Sooey and I'll stampede that herd. I'm thinking they'll follow the creek-run behind the house and down that little valley."

"Could be."

"You stay here and watch the place. When they ride out to head off the stampede, you hurry down there and set the charge."

"Suppose they don't ride out? Suppose they decide to let the stampede run the course? Suppose—"

"Jonah!"

We prepared the dynamite, tying six sticks in a bundle. "Better use a long fuse," Sis cautioned.

Upon completing the cap and fusing, Sis and Sooey mounted up. "We'll meet you back here, Jonah."

"When you get that herd running, you pull back, you hear? There's a lot of guns down there."

But she was already leaving. Pa always said Sis was long on opinion and short on heeding.

It came as thunder. First, screams sounding like a tree full of angry mama panthers broke the silence. Sooey could sound just like a panther and his voice sure could carry. Unless you knew he was about to break loose with it, it'd nearly send you into shock.

Two shots followed the panthers, and the heavy roar of a stampede rolled through the night. As Sis predicted, the cattle raced for the valley, shoving along the creek-run behind the house.

Men yelled as they poured out of the bunkhouse toward the horse corral. Several guarding the house hustled to join them.

With no time to waste, I headed down the hill, approaching the house from the creek side, keeping to the trees whenever possible. The frightened cattle were moving farther out along the valley.

The stallion snorted when I tied him and proceeded on foot. I ran toward the house, expecting a gun to flash in my face. Not all the guards had taken to saddle.

Behind the shack, I listened, catching my wind. Peeking around the corner, I saw a guard near the front corner of the house. He held the rifle ready, looking all around.

Slowly, I worked the lever of the Winchester. The well-oiled mechanism performed quietly.

Deciding to chance it, I made myself small while tiptoeing toward the door to the root cellar. The distant drumming of the stampede gave some comfort. At least the cattle had not, as yet, been turned.

I had to be quick about it. Voices sounded close. The hinges squeaked as I pulled open the heavy door and ducked in. I lowered it closed in a hurry.

Being on the top steps, I had to stoop low, my back touching the slantways door. I held my breath. They'd paused just outside. I dared not shift the rifle, not knowing what jar or bucket I might knock over.

"Dammit! I know I heard something back here," a guard proclaimed.

"Maybe we'd better check the cellar," said another.

"You check it. You couldn't hire me to go down there—not since the cook saw that big rattler."

One sat on the door. "Don't make sense. Trying to steal a herd from under our nose. You got the makings?"

"You know something, Slim?" one said after a while, lighting up. "They got guts, whoever they are. You have to give them that. Smith and Hollend could lose their grip on things."

"Naw. They'll get them. And when they do, out comes the whip."

The other one sat on the door. "Wonder who peeled ol' Brutus's scalp thataway?"

"I don't know, but it's too bad they didn't kill the son of a bitch."

"You know, I saw him drive a pick through a man at the mine. And that was after he'd nearly beat him to death with his fist."

"Tell you what I'm gonna do the next time he shoves me outa the way."

"What's that, Slim?"

"Shoot the bastard!"

The other chuckled, "I'd give a month's pay to see that. He's the only man I know who everybody hates."

My right foot was going to sleep. I tried to move it. The steps squeaked.

"What's that?"

"Ol' Tessie in the kitchen, probably."

"Now there's one who doesn't hate Brutus."

"'Cause he's the only man who can stomach her in bed."

The dank cellar smelled of rotten potatoes. Perspiration burned my eyes. The wet shirt stuck to my back. If the others returned anytime soon, it'd be too late and I'd be stuck in the cellar for no telling how long.

"We'd best check around, Slim. Besides, I don't relish sitting on this door. That bastard down there is big enough to bite through wood."

They moved away. I struck a match, trying to see what was below me. Empty sacks hung over a pole. Bins, some empty, lined one wall.

Careful where I put my feet, I moved quietly down the steps. When the match burned down, I had another ready, lighting it from the dying flame.

Something behind a basket on the floor moved. I stayed on

the bottom step. Carefully, I took the bundle of dynamite and gently placed it on the floor, near the step. The best place would be against the far wall, closer to the center of the house. I decided against going over there.

Unrolling the fuse, I strung it up the steps and lit it. Hurried voices came from around the front of the house. Some of the guards had returned!

Pushing up the door slightly, I let the fresh air fill my lungs. Boots sounded around the corner. I almost let the door drop. The fuse spurted brightly. I covered it with the tail of my coat, burning my hand in the process.

"Check the cellar!" ordered a voice from around front.

"I just did!" someone yelled back, running around the back of the house.

My coat smoldered. I dropped the hot fuse and beat the embers off with my hand. Something sizable crawled across the floor toward the steps. I was outside before I realized it. I shut the door, blocking out the light from the fuse. Three men carrying rifles made their way across the side yard. I ducked down near the door.

"Come on! You have fresh horses. Let's find 'em!"

They galloped off. I ran for the trees. Mounting, I kicked a heel against the stallion and held on.

Sis and Sooey sat on impatient horses at the top of the swell. "What kept you?" Sis demanded.

I wiped a palm across my forehead. My hands still trembled. "I'd rather not say."

She looked back at the house. At an upstairs window, Tessie stuck out her head. "Brutus!" She yelled toward the bunk-house. "You get up here! You promised. Your head can't still be hurtin' all that bad."

"How long was that fuse anyway, Jonah?"

"Real long," I said, nudging the stallion with my heel. He leaped forward.

We were at the bottom of the slope and headed for the fort

when the house went. Our horses never missed a stride. Later, some miles away, we looked back. The sky above the ranch was aglow.

"We'll blow the mine next," Sis advised.

"If we live," I replied.

# CHAPTER 10

THE odor of dog jerked me awake. I opened my eyes to see sharp white spikes in my face.

"I wouldn't make any sudden moves, boy," the old man warned from somewhere in the dark. "He's been a mite touchy the last few days."

I'd fallen asleep on watch. Day was breaking in the east.

"Mistake going to sleep like that, boy."

"You want to get this beast out of my face?" I asked, making certain I sounded friendly.

Sweetie growled. The old man snapped his fingers and the dog sat down against my rifle arm, his long tongue dripping on my neck.

"He's still in my face," I pointed out, politely.

At the cluck, Sweetie went to him. I sat up slowly. The old man stood in the shadows. Behind him, near the stallions, Sis turned under her blanket. Sooey snored.

"Falling asleep like that can be dangerous," he said. "If I was your enemy, your throat would be slit."

"By you or the dog?"

"What difference would it make? You'd be dead."

I blew my nose. "Your dog has bad breath."

"Mean is always bad. Breath ain't no exception."

Getting up, I placed sticks on the few dying embers. "You come out here to aggravate or what?"

"Mostly to check on things." The sticks soon caught and he limped to the fire, warming his bad leg. The air had a bite to it.

"Folks are funny. Townspeople are becoming upset—at least, some are. Those who have been helping Smith and

Hollend are growing concerned, wondering what'll happen to them when those two are no longer around."

"Like maybe settle-up time?"

He nodded, turning his other side to the fire. "Sitting around town, I hear most of the rumors. Talk going around is that maybe some of the people around here have had enough and are out to change things—like stampeding a herd or blowing up a house."

I squatted near the fire.

"That's what makes some nervous. Seems no one has considered the possibility that outsiders could be causing the trouble."

"Meaning us?"

"Who else?"

"We blowed the house," I said.

He turned the lame leg back to the fire. "Knew nobody else had the guts. Nor will they ever."

"You don't expect much from the people in Little Hope, do you?"

He studied me. "They've been accustomed to the ways of Smith and Hollend too long. You watch out for them. They could be your worst enemies. You know what to expect from Smith or Hollend. You can never know what the locals are capable of doing."

"You're saying they're all bad?"

"Didn't say that. But most of them are."

He saw that I was giving his words some thought.

"Leech was one of them," he added. "He was born here."

"Why are you helping us, old man?" I asked suddenly.

"I've got my own settling to do, boy. It'll all be clear in due time. Now, try to keep alert!"

He rode out, the dog loping ahead of the horse. I didn't tell Sis about the old man's visit. It would serve no good for her to learn I had fallen asleep on watch again. I promised myself it would not happen a third time.

In the afternoon, we started for town. We needed more fuse in order to blow the mine.

Leaving the saddles on, we put the three Winds in the last three stalls at the livery and fed them grain. The owner of the stable sat out in a chair propped against the front of the building. He ignored us.

The mine wagons rolled in. After the workers climbed out, one continued down the street, stopping in front of the S and H. The driver went inside.

We stepped back against the bank, letting three women and two men pass. Six riders came down the street and tied up in front of a small saloon. A woman, leaning against the porch post and wearing a see-much dress, followed them inside.

"The noise here is enough to make a person hate towns," Sis declared. "And look what they did to the church house!"

Horses crowded the rails at the front. Lights showed through the high windows. Women, some girls, went in. Their dresses were not the kind one wore to a Sunday meeting.

"You suppose they put up curtains inside?" I wondered.

"Heathens!" she said. "They probably do their laying out in the open."

We started past the S and H. Henry, talking to a cowboy on the porch, saw us. She motioned us over to the end of the porch.

"There's been a lot of questions and checking about," she said in a hushed tone. "People are scared. Hollend's men have been searching the prairie for two days."

"Do they know who they're looking for?" Sis hushed back.

"I don't think so. But sooner or later, they're bound to figure it out."

"Later, we'll be telling them ourselves," Sis said.

Henry saw me looking. She gave me a teasing smile and acted like she was trying to pull the top of her dress up to cover the smooth swells. "I just put on a pot of coffee."

Sis pulled the wide-brim down over her face and buttoned the coat. "Believe I'll have a cup, Henry."

We made it through the crowd to a table in back. Sooey adjusted the ax under his blanket-wrap and sat down, grinning. He'd drink coffee all day so long as it was strong and black.

Several miners stood with the ranch hands at the long polished bar. Two farmers at the next table spoke in low voices, worried about the weather and if there would be more order or disorder in the county.

Tobacco smoke, hanging like folds of clouds near the ceiling lamps, tainted the air. Men throughout the room spoke in low tones, sipping beer and whiskey.

Henry returned with a tray holding three cups of coffee. "I'd better mingle," she said, leaving us.

Sis turned pale. "That's him!" she whispered. "Oates Smith is at the end of the bar."

The coiled whip hung over his right shoulder and under his arm. His pink, stubby fingers held a shot glass to his mouth. His thick lips seemed to be kissing the rim of the glass as he sipped the red liquid.

Large, dull gray eyes stared from under the brown Stetson, dancing over the faces of others.

A long tan coat draped his round shoulders, making him appear shorter than he was. A black string tie hung outside his red vest.

Flabby jowls gave his round face a hoggish look. The trim, black mustache received constant caresses from his thumb. He seemed to prefer doing that over kissing the glass.

Now and then, he'd set the glass down and fondle the braided-leather whip handle, all the while dusting his shiny boots off against a pants leg.

His eyes met mine. I stared back through the smoke haze. My hand automatically went to the Winchester resting across my lap.

Suddenly, his eyes danced to someone else and he picked up the glass.

The bat-wing doors slammed open. Brutus came in, using his thick frame to shove people aside. He shuffled bow-legged to the bar, elbowed a cowboy out of the way, and took someone's bottle and glass.

The sleeves of the gray cotton shirt, rolled up to his elbows, revealed hairy, muscular arms. Halting, he looked around, taking in the room. The gash on his cheek made by my rifle barrel was a furrow in the thick black beard. His hat hid whatever mark I'd put in his scalp.

"Move!" he ordered us. "This is my table."

"Go to hell!" Sis said, without looking up.

He kicked the chair out from under her. She thumped to the floor, hard.

The bearlike sound gurgled out of Sooey between clenched teeth as he sprang to his feet. His right fist was almost touching the floor behind him when he began the swing.

I heard the air swoosh as the fist passed over my head. It crushed Brutus's flat, wide nose. Blood poured.

Brutus fell across the saloon against the bar, knocking men and bar over. Glasses and bottles smashed against the floor.

Sooey stood over Brutus when he rolled out onto the floor. With a left fist full of shirt, Sooey jerked him to his feet.

"Thonofbitch! You hurt Thister!" screamed the bear voice. He brought the edge of his fist down on top of Brutus's head, slamming him back to the floor.

Brutus shook his head, struggling slowly to his feet. Sooey stepped back, waiting and growling.

He landed a blow to Sooey's jaw, knocking him against the back wall. The building shook.

Sooey hurried back and they exchanged blows, standing flat-footed and close. Neither was quick, nor too concerned about blocking the other's blows.

Sooey short-jabbed a fist to Brutus's mouth. Brutus did the same to Sooey. Again, Sooey pounded with a short. So did Brutus. Both growled now.

Oates Smith's eyes moved back and forth between the two fighters. His hand milked the whip handle.

"I didn't hurt the bitch!" Brutus yelled.

Sooey reached all the way back, over his outstretched right leg. He bested Brutus in height, and when he swung, his fist caught Brutus under the chin, lifting him. He stumbled backward through the bat-wings.

Soon, the doors flew open and Brutus shuffled back in, his scowling face running into another floor-to-jaw sledgehammer. Back through the front door he tumbled.

It took him longer this time to pick himself up off the porch and throw open the doors. Blood covered his beard and shirt. Out from under curled lips, several teeth hung loosely in his bleeding gums.

Smith milked the whip handle all the more. A slight smile distorted the corners of his mouth.

The blow to Sooey's stomach came hard, bending him over. Then came a blow to his face. He fell to his knees. Brutus picked up a chair and broke it across Sooey's back. Brutus stepped back, breathing hard and reaching for another chair.

Sooey came off the floor, grabbing power with leg muscles and distance. Brutus's jaw cracked under the smashing fist. His legs trembled. He stumbled back, losing his bearing. Sooey rushed toward him, swinging a hard right. It landed solidly, sounding like a shot.

Brutus made a somersault through the door.

"Stop knocking him out the door, Big 'un," said a whisker-faced cowboy seated against the wall. "He's gonna wear out the hinges!"

"Yeah," his buddy chided. "Smack his ass through the window!"

Sooey did.

We waited. Outside, Brutus dragged something heavy out of a wagon. He kicked open the doors, holding a miner's pick. Blood trickled from cuts on his shoulder and arms.

"You might know the son of a bitch wouldn't have the decency to come in the way he went out," the cowboy remarked casually.

Brutus yelled obscenities, punctuated with "I kill! I kill!"

"Yeah. I bet," the cowboy scoffed.

He started for Sooey, swinging the pick as if it was a stick of firewood. The onlookers in the saloon huddled against the walls.

Sooey freed his ax, the thin edges of the double blade reflecting light from the lamps. Brutus pulled up abruptly, his eyes fixed on the blade. He seemed bewildered.

"Uh huh," the cowboy grunted. "There's a new picture on the wall."

Screaming, Brutus rushed forward, swinging the pick overhead and down. The point snagged Sooey's blanket-wrap, ripping a large hole and jerking him off balance.

Brutus moved in for the kill, bringing the pick up.

Sooey, one hand around the handle, swung the ax hard while trying to gain his balance.

The blade drove deep into Brutus's chest. He fell, legs buckling under him. Sooey returned the ax to his belt and found his hat.

"You killed him. You bury the bastard!" the bartender demanded.

"Go to hell!" bellowed Sooey.

Sis and I followed him out onto the porch. "Drinks on the house," the bartender announced. "Once the bar is upright."

Sis took Sooey's bruised hand in both of hers. She pressed it against her cheek. "You're a good friend, Sooey."

He took several deep breaths. Chuckling, he turned around, looking skyward. He almost fell off the porch.

The old man spoke from the darkness at the other end of the porch. "They brought your mule in a while ago," he said, voice low. "Had a dynamite box tied to the pack. One of them rode out to get Hollend."

A rider dismounted at the hitching rail, tied his horse, and stepped onto the porch.

"They'll have men at the fort waiting for you," the old man continued after the rider had entered the saloon. "Go to the other camp."

Sis turned in the direction of the livery. "Our horses!"

"I had them moved earlier to the stable behind the Dry Goods. If you need anything from the store, you'd better go get it. You don't have much time. Go around back. They're watching the street."

We rushed down the alley and along the rear of the buildings to the Dry Goods. At the corral at the rear of the livery stable, three men examined the horses.

Entering with the key, we closed the door behind us. I lifted a wooden box full of dynamite sticks and handed it to Sooey. He shoved it under his arm as if it had been a pillow. Sis grabbed a box of caps and I picked up a spool of fuse.

"Cartridges, Jonah," Sis reminded me.

I loaded my pockets with boxes of .44's and .45's from the shelf behind the counter. Outside the front door, two men with rifles paused. We ducked down. Someone down the street yelled. They hurried that way.

Sis padlocked the door. I moved toward the barn. The low growls stopped me. Sweetie stood in front of the stable door.

"Make him move, Jonah!" Sis whispered.

"How am I supposed to do that?"

*"Ssshhh!"*

Sweetie gave another hint of his determination to stay put. All along his neck and back the hair jumped straight up.

From the dark, a finger snapped and the dog stalked away. We led the horses out and mounted. A rifle cracked from the vicinity of the livery and the bullet jerked at my sleeve. Other shots followed, and the street became a canyon of yells and orders.

We headed in the direction of the fort. The stallions seemed thrilled over the possibility of a race.

Five miles from town, Sis slowed, turning west, down the middle of a stream. After a while, we left the runnel and rode a wide circle, heading back toward town.

Later, I found myself following her along the washout at the bottom of a slope. "You know where you are?" I said.

She dismounted. "Of course. A whorehouse used to be up there."

"We shouldn't have come here!"

"That's right, Jonah. Tell the whole town where we are!"

"We shouldn't have come here," I whispered.

"That's why we're here. No one will suspect that we circled back to town."

"Why?"

"Make up two bundles of dynamite with long fuses."

Sooey handed down the box. I took out my pocket knife and pried off the top. "How long you want the fuses?"

"Long enough for us to make it from the S and H saloon to that shack out back at this end of town."

"Will we be walking or running?"

"Jonah!"

"Running fuses, then."

I made up the bundles, five sticks to each. We sat down, leaning against the ditch, waiting for Little Hope to go to sleep.

"What else we blowing up besides the saloon, Sis?"

"That place where Smith and Hollend keep all their money."

"We're blowing up the bank?!"

# CHAPTER 11

LATER, on the knoll, we watched as Little Hope's lights gradually winked out. Three of the saloons, though, were still open.

"You know something, Jonah?" Sis said. "When this is over, I'd best start thinking about woman things."

"Like what?"

"Oh, you know. Husband, young'uns and such."

"I reckon."

"You think we should go back to Texas?"

"Seems like we should."

The lights went out in one of the saloons. "Of course, we could get us a little place—the three of us—and make do just fine," Sis went on.

"We could," I admitted. "It'd give you plenty of time to husband-hunt."

"I don't intend making it a hunt, Jonah! When I see my man, I'll know it. We'll court a decent spell and then marry."

"Sounds proper enough."

"Of course it is! When a woman finds the man she wants, she should get him to thinking about settling down. A woman doesn't enjoy sleeping alone on a cold night either."

She stood up, tugging and adjusting her long coat.

"Sis, I thought we were going to blow the mine."

"We are, but we have to take our opportunities where and when we find them."

"Well, we might miss this one if we don't soon move. That bunch looking for us could be returning anytime."

All lights were out except at the S and H Saloon and at the marshal's office. The light always burned at night in the marshal's office. The banker, according to the marshal, preferred it that way, saying it gave townfolk a feeling of security.

"Let's go," Sis said.

"But there's still people in the saloon!"

"We go anyway. It'll be daybreak before we know it. By the time we get things ready at the bank, everyone should be gone from the saloon."

We left Sooey holding the horses behind the shanty and advanced to the rear of the bank. There was no window, and the thick, wooden door was not one we could break in. We moved quickly down an alley to the street.

The old lock was difficult. With my pocket knife, I finally worked the latch and pushed the door open. We darted in.

The large safe took up most of the wall behind the teller's cage. The banker's office was at the rear, enclosed by a railing.

"It'll take more'n five sticks to blow that safe open, Sis."

"We didn't come here to steal," she whispered. "Just blow the building."

I had an idea. I stuck the end of the fuse out under the bottom of the front door and carried the bundle of dynamite behind the teller's cage and shoved it under the safe.

"There," I said. "All we have to do is run down the walk and light the fuse from outside."

"By damn, Jonah! You're getting good at this sort of thing."

The street was clear. We stepped onto the walk. I closed the door, pulling out a couple inches of fuse.

At the alley next to the saloon, we looked in through the window. Two cowboys—or gang members more'n likely—were at a table with a bottle. The bartender, seated at a table nearby, dozed with his head on his arm.

"They don't look like they're fixing to leave anytime soon, Sis."

She sighed, leaning her back against the building. "What are we going to do?"

"I don't know. It'll be daylight soon."

She grabbed my arm. "Horses?"

I listened. We'd tarried too long!

Five galloped into town, their riders dismounting in front of the saloon. The bartender got up and went behind the bar.

"Find them?" a cowboy at the table asked.

"Lost their trail. We came back for fresh horses." He turned up a glass. "But we'll get them. Be day soon."

I spoke in Sis's ear. "We'd better get moving."

"Not yet. I've an idea." She pulled me down the alley to the rear of the building.

"Listen. I'll go light the fuse at the bank, get Sooey and the horses, and wait for you over there near the shanties."

"But—"

She jerked on my sleeve. "When the bank blows, they'll run out and down there. You throw the dynamite in the saloon."

"But—"

"Be sure you cut the fuse short, though."

"But suppose they don't run out?"

"Throw it anyway. Just be sure you use a *real* short fuse. You don't want them to throw it back at you."

Before I could say anything more, she was running down the alley. I moved to the corner.

I couldn't see her on the dark walk. With my knife, I cut the long fuse and dug for matches. I held the knife ready in the event I'd need a shorter fuse.

She struck the match. It seemed to light up the entire town. The fuse caught, spurting. I rushed down the alley and around to the back of the saloon. Gently, I tried the back door. It refused to budge. I decided the front door would have to do.

The Winchester felt heavy. Wiping my hands on my coat, I slipped alongside the building to the front corner.

Squatting, I waited, dynamite, matches, knife, and rifle all ready. Of course, I had to hold the knife between my teeth. Sweat rolled off my nose.

I'd decided the fuse must've gone out just when the bank finally went. The saloon shook. The street filled with flying splinters, stones, and roof. For an instant, the entire town was lit up bright as day.

They poured out of the saloon, running down the street. Jumping to my feet, I ran in. Putting the bundle on the floor behind the bar, I struck the match, holding it to the fuse. When it caught, I hurried out.

I hugged the front wall, cleared the steps, and made a dash for the shanties.

The three Winds hit full stride as the saloon exploded. The walls flew out. The roof, or what was left of it, caved in.

Sis headed toward the road to the mine. Gaining it, we traveled a mile before turning off onto the road leading to Morely's Settlement a few miles north. When we turned toward our new camp, the sun was high in the morning sky.

Nearing the old homestead, we took to the stream, walking our horses as quietly as possible. The barn was larger than the house. Both soddies appeared ready to collapse. We put the horses in the small corral joining the shed side of the barn.

The house set under a big cottonwood. The old man had supplied the place well; grain for the horses and rations for us. He'd even sent along a double-barreled shotgun and two boxes of shells.

Sis and Sooey unrolled their blankets under the tree and were immediately asleep. I stood watch, walking about to stay awake. After four hours I awoke them, handed Sooey my rifle, and stretched out on Sis's blanket.

When Sooey awoke me four hours later, I smelled supper cooking. Sis'd kept the fire small under the pan. The thin trail of smoke dispersed among the branches overhead.

"Thought I'd fix supper before it rained," she said, moving the coffeepot closer to the fire.

The sky had turned dark with rolling clouds. I went into the house for the double-barrel and shells. Sis watched quizzically as I walked to the barn. When I returned to the fire, she was filling our plates. Sooey stood by impatiently.

"The shotgun and shells are hid under the straw with the dynamite," I said.

She handed me a plate. "Better get started on this. The rain won't hold off much longer."

"The barn is better shelter, Sis. Plenty of straw for bedding down too. Besides, we need to stay near the horses—just in case."

We set to eating. Not far away, a jagged streak of lightning probed at the ground, sizzling like frying side-meat. A roll of thunder bounced off the prairie. Wind gusted through the trees. "There's hail in those clouds," Sis predicted.

Large drops of rain spattered on the brim of her hat. Hearing the approaching horse, I picked up the rifle and stepped behind the tree. Sis and Sooey ran for the barn.

Henry rode in fast. She was soaking wet. "The damn rain followed me," she said, swinging down. Sweetie warned me with unpleasant sounds, shaking water over me.

"Put your horse in the corral," I yelled as hail rattled against the branches. I grabbed the hot coffeepot and followed.

"Better get out of them wet clothes," Sis advised Henry, handing her a blanket.

She went over in a corner behind us and stripped. Sis hung the wet clothes over a stall partition. Henry joined us on the straw, holding the blanket tightly around her.

She accepted the cup of coffee Sis offered, shivering. The dog lay near the door, protesting throatily at the hail bouncing on the ground near his feet.

"Riding out here was dangerous," Sis said.

"Not with Sweetie along."

"I meant for us."

"The old man sends me riding every day; mostly out of town a few miles and back. No one suspects anything when I leave town."

"What's the old man to you?" Sis said.

"Nothing," she replied, holding the cup to her lips with both hands. The short blond hair curled tightly all over her head. "He pays well, that's all."

"He pay you to sleep with him?" Sis asked straight out.

"No, he wouldn't do that. He treats me like I was his daughter." She shivered again, gulping down a swallow of coffee.

The hail pounded against the shingles. Thunder rolled in from two directions, seeming to collide overhead. Sooey lay back on the straw, looking at the low ceiling while he chewed.

"He wants to know what happened to the money," Henry said.

"What money?" I asked.

"The bank money."

"We didn't take any money from the bank," Sis said.

"It's gone. They found the safe on its side with the bottom blown out. The banker said all the money was stolen."

"Jonah, you said the dynamite wouldn't blow that safe."

I shrugged. "Must've had a weak bottom."

Sis explained what happened. "And if the money is gone, then they stole it!"

"They think you all took it, and there are several groups out hunting for you right now." She pulled the blanket closer around her.

"Was the bank destroyed?" I wanted to know.

"Yes, and the buildings on each side of it."

It turned cold. Sooey pulled up his blanket. Sis refilled our cups. We'd best stay alert, Jonah."

"They won't be out searching far tonight. Not in this weather."

"They're going to shoot you on sight, Jonah," Henry said. "They plan to put Sooey to work in the mine and Sis in the church house—which isn't a church anymore."

"We have different plans," Sis said evenly.

"The whole town's gone crazy," said Henry, her teeth chattering. She stretched out over a layer of straw, continuing to shiver. "I'm freezing, Sis," she chattered.

Sis was silent for a while. "Jonah, stretch out against her. Hold her close to you under your blanket."

"Huh?"

"She has to be kept warm, and we sure can't build a fire in here."

"How can I keep her warm?"

"Jonah!"

"*You* lie down next to her," I suggested.

*"Jonah!"*

I looked at Sis. She meant it. I looked at Henry. She shivered and nodded. "It'd warm me some, Jonah."

Lying down beside her, I covered us both with my blanket and put my arms around her, holding her close.

After a while, the shivering eased, but not much.

"Feel better?" Sis asked.

"A little. I'm not so cold now."

"Just stay close together," Sis advised. "You'll soon get warm."

The hail pelted the roof. Sweetie moved away from the door, coming to lay down near me, exchanging growls for raised bristles.

Quickly, I moved closer to Henry, away from him. She slid an arm around me, her nose against my neck, nudging.

"How do you feel now, Henry?" Sis asked from under her blanket in the far corner.

"A little better, Sis," she said softly. "If I could just get warm." She shivered again.

"You must be real feverish," Sis replied.

"I think I am."

"Is Jonah giving off much heat?"

"A little—I think."

I was sweating. In a stall, one of the stallions stomped a foot. Sweetie turned his head, growling against the back of my neck.

Henry twisted, seeming to want to get closer. "I'll never feel warm again," she declared.

"Hold her closer, Jonah," Sis advised.

She couldn't get any closer. She rolled over and my hand touched bare back. She shivered, moaning and twisting against me.

"You keep a level head, Jonah," Sis said sleepily, over the sound of the hail, "or I'll tell the redhead."

Henry's breast sent little tingles across my chest. A knee moved up over my thigh. She made a little cry and I couldn't tell if she was asleep or not. The worst of the shivers seemed to have passed, however.

When I moved back a little, Sweetie growled into my ear and the cold tip of his nose touched my neck. I jumped.

Henry breathed deeply, nudging her chin against my throat. I tried to move my arm. Somehow, my hand ended up touching her bare thigh. She moved the knee along my leg again, so I just let my hand rest where it was, seeing it didn't seem to bother her any.

It was getting warmer under the blanket. When I figured she was finally asleep, I tried to turn over, but Henry moved her leg all the way over me.

I slid a hand down to gently move it. It was heavy as a log. She moaned and twisted again, taking my hand and moving it to a firm, smooth buttock. Her face pressed against my neck, her breath tickling me.

Later, she stretched and shifted. Before I knew it, my face was buried in her large, soft breasts, a nipple throbbing against my eye.

I lay there, Henry moaning and Sweetie breathing on the back of my neck. Henry's leg came back over mine as she nudged close again.

The hail changed to rain. I listened to it running off the roof for a while. I sat up, planning to take my blanket elsewhere. Henry turned onto her back. A flash of lightning revealed the whole naked length of her.

She roused slightly. "I'm cold, Jonah," she mumbled.

I lay back down, pulling the blanket over us. She twisted and grunted close. In a minute or two, she rolled over, her back against me. She searched for and found my arm, pulling it around her, pressing my hand to her breast. When she sounded asleep, I tried to move it. She grunted and pulled it back, cuddling her rump up closer.

Sweetie never growled when she moved. Only when I did. I stayed still for a long time.

Henry was soft as you please. She put my hand back on her buttock and twisted and squirmed all about, shoving her leg all the way over me. She hardly shivered at all anymore. I was throbbing and had the worst headache.

I finally cleared my face from the hollow of her breasts and freed my hand from her rear. Sweetie growled the whole time but I managed to move slightly away from Henry.

A lot of good it did! She just slid over, her arm going around my neck and a heavy leg draping over me, holding me fast like a vise. I tried to ease back, but Sweetie decided he'd been tolerant long enough. He growled his low warning in my ear. I lay real still.

When Henry settled down again and I no longer felt Sweetie's mean breath on my neck, I tried slipping out from under her leg and the blanket.

It didn't work. The dog made a low, meaningful noise and Henry moaned, pulling my face back against her breast. She hugged the leg over me tightly, sighing some. I didn't sleep a wink the whole blessed night!

The morning came clear and cool. Sis cooked a big breakfast and we sat near the fire, finishing up with a second cup of coffee.

Sitting with Sis on the other side of the fire, Henry looked over the rim of her cup at me.

"You sleep well, Jonah?" Sis wanted to know.

Henry sipped her coffee, her eyes holding me. "Storm kept me awake," I said, drinking more coffee.

"I had nice dreams—about Jonah," Henry said, getting up. "I have to go now."

When she was in the saddle, she reined the horse over near me. "You're lucky I had a fever."

"No, I wasn't."

Her eyes ran over me. “Come on, dog!” she called to Sweetie, jerking her horse around.

Sis came to stand behind me as I watched her riding off. “Go get some sleep. We’ll wake you at sundown.”

“What about the mine?”

“We’ll see about it tonight.”

I headed for my blanket in the barn.

# CHAPTER 12

THE mine entrance, a black hole at the bottom of a long grade, stared back at us like a one-eyed beast. Locals referred to the area as "hill country." Sprawling mounds seesawed across the grassy prairie for miles.

The moon was a peach slice of yellow, offering some light on the scene below. The tool shack made a leaning sentry near the entrance. A light streamed from a larger building a hundred yards away. A long shed formed part of the fence to the corral near by. Mules milled about in the corral and shed. Two freight wagons, loaded with coal, waited at the end of the steel tracks emerging from the mine.

We lay in the tall grass, watching as men with rifles shifted about.

"They're expecting us," Sis said, pushing the wide-brim back on her head. I studied the outline of her nose.

"How we going to set the dynamite with so many men about?"

"I'm thinking on it, Jonah."

I turned on my back, put my hands under my head, and crossed one leg over the other. Sometimes Sis gave a thing a lot of thought.

"Could always shoot our way in," she speculated.

"Getting out might be a problem, though," I reminded her.

She gave me a hard look. Sooey turned on his back, cupping his hands under his head. He propped big shoes on the dynamite box. He chewed in deep thought.

"I count five men down there," she said after a while.

"Could be others in the building, too."

"I know that!"

The air was cool. Some sort of little animal darted through the tall grass a few feet away. One of the guards at the mine had a displeasure of some kind and yelled his opinion at another.

"Foul mouth," Sis mumbled.

"He doesn't know you're about, Sis."

She cast me another look. Sooey turned his head and spat a stream.

"Sure pleasant out here," I offered.

Sis grunted. "Would you like me to fetch you a cup of coffee?"

I never talked back when she had a snappish tone in her voice. Anyway, she was trying to think.

My thoughts focused on Henry. I was looking forward to growing up. Having shared a blanket with a naked woman all night put pleasurable thoughts in a man's head. She sure was soft. Smelled pretty, too. If only—

"What are you breathing so hard about?" Sis demanded.

I looked at the slice of peach overhead.

"Reckon we could slip into that mine without them seeing us?" she wondered aloud.

"Don't see how we could do that."

"Maybe if we started shooting, they'd leave."

"No, they wouldn't."

"We might be able to draw them—"

"Wouldn't work, either."

"Jonah!" She hit me with her hat. "You get up from there and at least act like you're helping!"

I got up and took out several sticks of dynamite. "What are you doing?" she asked.

"Making some bundles."

"You've an idea?"

"Which way is the wind blowing?" I said.

She pointed toward the mine. "Why?"

"If this grass was set fire, it'd head for them buildings down there. Keep them occupied for a while, wouldn't it?"

She jumped up. "That might work!"

"Only thing is, the whole prairie will burn for miles."

"Who gives a damn!"

"I guess the streams and creeks will eventually stop it, though."

She kneeled down next to the box of explosives and began helping. "You think the fire will travel as far as our camp?"

"Not likely. Too many runnels between here and there."

"Better make long fuses," she cautioned. "What about our horses? You think about that?"

"When we set the fire, we'll head for that big washout down yonder and leave Sooey with the horses while we work our way toward the mine on foot."

"That's a lot of open ground from the ravine to the mine, Jonah!"

"They'll be busy keeping the fire from the mules and buildings."

"If we get caught in that clearing, we won't have a chance."

"We sure wouldn't, so we'd best not get caught there."

She put a hand on mine. "I'm scared, Jonah."

"So am I," I admitted.

Sis carried a bundle of six sticks and I took the other two. Behind the crest, we set a stretch of fire and rushed to the ravine. The grass caught quickly, the wind whipping it along. The men guarding the mine began shouting at one another.

The horses went down into the ravine, sliding and groping for footing. Behind us, the sky was turning to an orange glow as the fire roared.

We let the horses pick their way until the gulley began shallowing out. Sis and I went ahead on foot.

We paused at the edge of the clearing. The rapidly approaching flames lit up the whole area. A guard screamed at the mules, herding them toward the corral gate. Others throwed buckets of water against the rear of the larger building.

"Now!" I told Sis, taking a firm grip on the Winchester.

We ran. Sis's holster slapped against her leg as she bounded across the clearing.

Inside the entrance, she paused, gasping for air and tugging at her britches. She'd almost lost them.

The two throwing water on the building yelled for the others to bring more water. The sky filled with smoke and embers.

The glow cast a somber light along the long tunnel ribbed with heavy timbers. Quickly, we moved deeper into the mine. Where the tunnel branched, we set the first charge with the longest fuse against the braces. Putting a match to it, Sis and I ran toward the entrance.

Halfway, we put a bundle against a beam. When the fuse spurted, we rushed to place the third charge.

"I hope you made those fuses long enough, Jonah," Sis worried as we ran toward the entrance.

A few feet inside the opening, I pushed the dynamite between two heavy posts. Sis was already moving when the fuse caught.

A bullet smacked the wall near my head. We ducked back in. The rifle cracked from behind one of the freight wagons as two more shots blasted, sending lead ricocheting down the mine tunnel.

"Jonah?"

I fired two quick ones at where I thought the shooter hid. Rifle fire responded. Sis drew her pistol and fired.

"We're in a mess, Jonah!"

One of the water bearers at the building dropped his bucket and picked up a rifle. He came running to help. My bullet slapped him southwards.

The rifle at the wagon kept us clinging to the ground. Behind us, the fuses burned brightly.

"We have to do something, Jonah!"

I wiped a sleeve over my face. Pictures of Jane, naked and preening in a stream, welled up in my mind. Every curve and swell was covered with droplets of water. Sunshine sparkled off her pinkish body. I knew I wasn't ready to die.

*"Jonah!"*

"Keep him pinned down," I heard myself telling Sis. "I'll try to make it to the wagon."

She began firing. I dashed forward, running for the rear of the wagon. The fire had reached the building. The men gave up trying to protect it. They ran toward the mine with their rifles.

Someone saw me as I darted around the wagon. His rifle was turning to me as I fired. My shot caught him in the chest.

"Run!" I yelled at Sis.

The others stopped to empty their guns at us. One fired at Sis as she ran toward the ravine. My bullet took a chunk out of his shoulder.

Firing two quick shots at the others, I ran. Bullets whizzed by my ear. One tore at the trailing end of my coat. I caught up with Sis as we sped out of the clearing.

The explosions came in quick succession. Coal, dust, and timber belched from the mine as the earth trembled.

Fire was everywhere now, spreading out fast. The heavy, acrid air filled my nostrils. My eyes burned.

Sooey mounted. I handed him the dynamite box. He tucked it under his arm. Sis rode out through the smoke. "Hurry, Jonah! We're about to get cut off!"

The fire held by the ravine, but there was nothing to stop it up ahead from completely blocking us in.

We just made it ahead of the flames. Behind us, the fire spread far across the prairie. Windswept, the orange tongues licked toward the sky.

It wasn't long before we came to a creek. Here the fire could go no farther unless sparks jumped across to the other side. We let the horses drink before crossing.

Once, almost running into a group of riders, we slowed the horses, keeping alert.

Toward dawn, we watered and rested. The expansive horizon behind glowed under a shelf of thick smoke.

The wind shifted, blowing down from the north, carrying the fire and smoke toward Little Hope.

"Where's the Lazy T spread from here, Jonah?" Sis asked.

"I think we're on it."

"Can you think of any good reason why Smith and Hollend should have all this grass when others don't?"

"Not a one."

She struck a match to a dry clump of grass.

We mounted up and headed northeast, planning to ride a wide loop to camp. Keeping to the high ground, we let the stallions find their own gait.

We rode right into our enemies.

# CHAPTER 13

WE topped the hill just as they were galloping up the other side. One led a horse carrying two women. The dress of the youngest was ripped off a shoulder.

Out of the eight men, three appeared to be townfolk. The others, degenerates no doubt, worked for Smith or Hollend or both.

Their guns came out. I fired as we reined about. The lead man toppled from the saddle, firing his six-shooter into the ground.

We were racing down the hill before they organized. Pistol and rifle shots filled the air. Bullets flew all around us.

The stallions went to work, gathering speed. Sooey held onto the box of explosives, his blanket-wrap waving behind him. Sis made a small target as she rode bent over in the saddle.

They fell back, their mounts no match for our horses. Later, when we came to a patch of trees, Sis guided her stallion into a swing to the right, down a rise and westerly—back in the direction from which we'd just come.

Nearing the top of a high point, we dismounted and gave the reins to Sooey. I followed Sis on foot to the crest.

They were turning back. I did not see the women. "We'll trail along behind them," Sis said.

"We will?"

"That bunch was out looking for us and come upon those women someplace. By damn, they treat women around here as if they were no more than stray cows, free for the taking!"

"Wonder where the women are?"

"Wherever it is they're going. They left a man with them when they came after us."

She went to her horse. Sooey shifted the box of sticks to his other arm and we rode on.

Just after dark we came up on them. The fire of the camp showed through the trees some distance ahead. Tying our horses among the bush, we headed toward the camp on foot, keeping to the thick growth of cottonwoods and small oaks along the dry creek bed.

The growth thinned out and we moved silently from behind one tree to the other until we neared the camp. We took position behind a rotting tree trunk.

They'd made camp in an open area near the bank of the creek. The two women huddled close at the fringe of the firelight.

Three men sitting near the captives passed a bottle around. Another attended the coffeepot. Eventually, I accounted for all but one.

A short bearded man appeared to be the leader. He spoke to the two standing nearby, and they dragged the women toward the fire.

The leader grabbed the front of the younger one's dress, ripping it open. She tried to cover herself, but he forced her hands down.

The others moved in closer to look. One snatched at the dress of the other girl. She stood bare to the waist.

"Strip!" ordered the leader.

They hesitated. He slapped the younger one, almost knocking her down. She could not have been more than sixteen.

When they had obeyed, the men gathered around, touching, fondling, laughing.

Two began pulling at the younger one, arguing. Their curses grew louder. The leader kicked at one of them and he sulked back.

Several filled their cups with coffee and watched the women while the discussion continued as to who'd take what turn with which woman.

The townsman in the dark suit lit a cigar. He ran an arm

around the young brunette, cupping a breast in his hand. He spoke in her ear and she spat in his face.

He pressed the hot end of the cigar to her back. She screamed. He grabbed her arm, trying to keep her still while holding the cigar against a breast.

"Kill him, Jonah!"

As my sights lined up, a streak of gray leaped from the shadows, jaws clamping around the townsman's throat.

His screams, mingled with ferocious growls, stunned the camp. As Sweetie's fangs gnashed and ripped, a gang member raised the barrel of his rifle high, ready to swing it against the dog's head.

The beast sprang at his throat before he could bring the rifle down. Another pulled a pistol to shoot Sweetie. A shotgun blasted from the trees on the other side of the camp, carrying him ten feet.

Guns at the camp exploded in the direction of the blast. Sooey's panther scream sent chills up my spine, just about piercing my eardrums.

The leader swung his rifle in our direction, firing wildly. I squeezed one off to his center. The .44 slammed him across the fire, knocking over the coffeepot.

Sis shot the one nearest us in the foot as my bullet tore through his gut.

One ran for his horse. A shotgun cut him down. The last one threw down his pistol, trying to surrender. It didn't work. The buckshot blasted through his chest.

We approached the camp cautiously. The two women, dazed, stood frozen where they were when Sweetie leaped from the dark. Sis found blankets to cover them.

The old man limped into view. Sweetie stood over his last victim, blood on his jaws and spattered over his chest.

"Jonah! You're bleeding!" Sis yelled.

"Huh?"

She led me over to the fire. Blood dripped from my left hand. She gently removed my coat.

I then felt the pain shoot through my arm. Things began fading to black before my eyes.

"Better sit down, boy," the old man advised.

Sooey eased me to the ground. The bullet had ripped a gash in the muscle as it passed. The old man left, returning with his horse. He took a bottle of whiskey from the saddlebags and poured generously into the wound. I nearly came to my feet. I was proud I didn't give in to the sudden urge to scream.

The older woman, who appeared no more than twenty, tore off a strip of petticoat and fixed a bandage around my arm. Her hand shook terribly, but she was gentle.

Both she and the younger one were, I thought, clean-faced and comely. They and Sis fussed over me a good while.

"Just a scratch," said the old man. "He'll heal soon enough."

"I feel wobbly," I said.

"Well, you just sit there awhile," Sis said soothingly, patting me on the back.

"Yes," added the girl. "We don't want the bleeding to start up again."

Sooey brought several blankets, stretched them out near the fire and rolled one for a pillow. He lifted me gently onto the blankets. The old man sipped at his bottle, mouth primed for a grin.

"Must have been worse than I thought," he said dryly.

"It does pain some," I admitted.

"So does a stumped toe."

"How'd you chance to be here?" I asked.

"Jonah, don't you tax yourself with all that talk," Sis ordered.

Sweetie stretched out on the blankets beside me, grumbling in my face.

"Seeing the country," the old man answered, straining to lower himself to a squatting position on the other side of the dog. He took another nip from the bottle. "Care for a swig? Might ease all that suffering."

"Don't you dare, Jonah!" Sis said from where she was helping the women gather their clothes.

"How come you tryin' to burn up Kansas?" he asked.

"Seemed a good idea," I replied.

He grunted. "And the mine?"

"Blowed."

He grunted again, his gray eyes searching my face. "Smith and Hollend will be hard to get to. Both stay surrounded by gunnies day and night now."

"Like those dead around us?" said Sis, poking up the fire for more light.

"We were lucky these went down so quick," he said.

Sis examined my bandage. The old man sipped again. "Men are everywhere looking for you three. Better move only at night, but you need to get on with it."

"We're working up to that," Sis said.

"Not much of theirs left to destroy," he advised.

"There's the church building and that other large saloon," Sis told him.

He nodded. "Yeah, there's that. Didn't think you'd go so far as to blow up a church, though."

"It used to be a church," Sis corrected. "It's a whorehouse now."

He struggled to his feet. "I won't argue against that." He looked down at me. "Know what you plan for Oates Smith and Marvin Hollend, boy. I don't think it'll work. Hollend doesn't wear that cut-down holster for nothing. He's been up against some mean ones and he's always walked away. You don't have to face him, you know."

"Fletchers give equals," I said.

"His kind doesn't deserve an equal chance. Shoot him down the first chance you get, I say."

"Jonah is the head of what's left of this Fletcher family," Sis stated. "We buried our pa and sister because of them. Fletchers have always rendered their settlements out in the open in a draw-down."

"And if Jonah dies?"

"Then they'll have to kill me, too!"

He looked at us both. "Anyone ever tell you that Fletchers are stubborn?"

"All the time," Sis said, her head tilted back. "What is it to you, anyway?"

He grunted. "I'll see the women to home. You think you're well enough to ride, boy?"

I detected something besides concern in his tone. "I can ride."

"Good. Likely to get yourself shot again, lying about."

They moved out, with Sweetie running circles around them. Probably looking for another throat to open.

"How do you feel?" Sis asked when I stood up.

"I'm steady now."

"You sure?"

"I'm sure."

She handed me the Winchester. "Sooey will carry you if you like."

"I'm shot in the arm, Sis. Not in the foot."

"Just the same, you be careful."

I looked at her. She gently touched my arm. "You're all the family I have left, Jonah. You don't know how much you mean to me."

"I know," I said.

She blew her nose into a red bandanna. "After you've rested a few days, we'll finish it, Jonah. We'll get them both."

It would be finished, but I wasn't too sure who would do the getting. Actually, I wasn't too keen on giving them equals.

# CHAPTER 14

MY wounded arm hurt some, but after a day of lying around camp doing nothing, I was glad to be on the stallion again, pain or not.

Sis carried a long-fused bundle of five sticks of dynamite in her coat pocket. I had a similar bundle in mine. Ten sticks remained in the box hid in the barn.

When we neared the Lazy T, the prairie was a black smudge as far as you could see. The fire left little grass anywhere. A haze hung over the land. Our horses kicked up ash-dust as they moved along in a trot.

Midnight found us on the knoll, overlooking Little Hope's busy street. A crowd, some holding torches, milled near the mercantile at this end of the town.

Four men hung from the porch, their bodies like ghostly ornaments in a nightmare. At the church building at the other end of the town, windows glared yellowish at the dead.

People moved along the walk and street, forming long, slow-moving shadows. A few carried rifles.

We picked a bad night, Sis."

"Maybe not. With all the people about, they might not notice us. Let's go down and look around."

"Huh?"

"We might find a way to place the charges."

"Those men with rifles are guards!"

"That's why we should sneak in now. Later, when everyone leaves, they'll be watching every approach and movement."

"What makes you think they're not watching now?"

"They might be, but there's too many coming and going for them to pay much attention to two more," she reckoned.

"You think so?"

She lifted her chin. "We're fixing to find out."

"I don't see how being amongst all them folks is going to keep us from being shot. Someone's bound to recognize us."

"We're not going to parade down the street announcing ourselves, Jonah!"

"Look, Sis, I—"

"My mind's made up, Jonah. It's best we get on down there."

"And how you figure for us to place the charges and get out once everyone's gone? There's men watching all over the place."

"We'll think of something."

Leaving Sooey to guard the horses, we started down the knoll. We approached the livery stable from the rear, pausing at the corral to see if we could detect any movement behind the buildings.

Satisfied that no one was there, we crouched along to the back of the livery and entered the door carefully, our guns ready.

No one was inside, and we moved to the front door, being careful to keep out of the light streaming in from the torches. Across the street, several huddled near the hanging bodies. I recognized two of the hung men as the cowboys who were in the S and H the night we blowed the bank and saloon.

"Guess they found out who took the bank money, Sis."

She put a finger to her lips. "Quiet."

Two rifle toters walked by the livery, on down the street.

"We'll cross the street one at a time," she said.

"How come we need to be over there?"

"Because the saloon we're going to blow up is on that side of the street!"

"I know where the saloon is! But why not cross the street down yonder where it's dark?"

"Because no one'll pay us any mind if we cross out in the open in all that light."

"They won't?"

"Cover me," she said, walking out of the livery and across the wide, torch-lit street as if she didn't have an enemy in the whole state of Kansas. A man carrying a shotgun stood in the middle of the street. He was looking past her, down the road leading into town.

She walked by the group near the mercantile and on around to the back of the building.

When I stepped out into the light, my feet itched to run. The rifle rested uncommitted in the crook of my arm while my hands sweated.

One of the townsmen at the huddle spoke to me as I passed. I grunted and walked on, my feet itching all the more.

Sis tried to hide her smug look under the drooped widebrim. "See?" she said—though I noticed the Colt was ready in her hand.

I decided not to let her see me wipe a hand over my forehead. "That's a wide street," I allowed.

"It is that," she agreed.

Keeping close to the buildings, we scurried around the litter to the back of the saloon. Bits of conversation and laughter sifted through the rear door.

"See if it's locked," Sis said.

I stepped down to the door. The knob turned grudgingly. A hinge shrieked as I cracked it open. The back room was dark. A strip of light showed under the door to the main saloon.

"Someone's coming," Sis whispered, pushing me inside, ahead of her. She quickly closed the door. Outside, footsteps approached the rear of the saloon and continued on. We began to breathe again.

When our eyes grew accustomed to the dark, we found we were in a small room that served as storage and saloon office. Boxes of whiskey were stacked on the floor. More boxes were against the wall.

"Jonah, why can't we do here what we did at the bank?" she whispered in my ear.

"You mean run the fuse out under the door for lighting later?"

"It might save us a lot of trouble."

I took the bundle from my pocket and moved behind the boxes. Something broke the stream of light coming under the door. The knob turned. Sis ducked around behind the boxes, almost knocking me over.

Two men came in, leaving the door ajar. Light washed the room. We huddled close. Sis's foot pinned my rifle to the floor!

One of them lifted a box from the stack at our heads. "The back door's unlocked," he said.

"Damn swamper! I keep warning him about that!" He snapped the padlock in place. "I'm going to fire that bastard yet."

They carried out two boxes, closing the door. "By damn!" Sis muttered.

"We're in a mess," I said.

"Maybe there's a key in here someplace."

We couldn't find one. We searched the rolltop desk and the walls, feeling everywhere. Noise in the saloon became louder. The bartender returned for another case of whiskey. We ducked behind the boxes just in time. I was careful to keep the Winchester from under Sis's foot.

She remained silent for a while. "Run that fuse under the door, Jonah."

I shoved the end of the fuse through the crack, pushing out several inches. Stretching it as far as I could along the wall, I placed the dynamite behind a box.

"How are we going to get out of here, Jonah?"

"We might have to wait until everyone leaves and go out the front door."

"It'll be padlocked from the outside!"

"We'll just have to break a window or something," I ventured.

"That'll bring every guard in town on the run!"

"If there was a crowbar handy, we could loosen the hasp."

"We'd best come up with a better idea," she sighed. "Doubtful they'd keep a crowbar in a saloon."

The door opened. I held the rifle ready. A box slid off the stack with a grunt and the bartender closed the door behind him.

"They keep that up and we won't have anything to hide behind," Sis grumbled.

Quietly, I moved a box where I could sit and watch the door over the top of the stack. An hour passed. In the saloon some gambled, some drank, all got louder as time passed. Now and then, a woman's husky voice sounded a vulgarity.

"Hussy!" Sis declared.

Two men slipped into the storeroom, closing the door quickly. One made water near the back wall. "Damn Hollend anyway!" he growled. "He promised we'd get rich here. Everything's being blowed up or burned down."

"We still have that bank money, Hawk."

"That's another thing. Hollend nor Smith had the right to hang anybody!"

"Keep it down, Hawk!"

"Get the money. We're pulling out. I ain't staying with yahoos who can't get rid of a couple kids and a clod. Everybody saying it's those damn Fletchers."

"Well, whoever it is, they'll catch them soon enough and things'll be back like they were."

"Have you tallied the dead lately?" Hawk grunted. "Hell, for all we know, there's dynamite with a short fuse in this saloon right now!"

"They wouldn't dare come into town with so many guns showing."

"Yeah? Well, I heard what those Fletcher kids did at Timber Creek. If they're related to Harlan Fletcher—and they must be—just you think on what'll happen if ol' Harlan and his bad-ass boys ride into town. Those damn Fletchers stick closer than molasses on a cold plate!"

"Probably no kin."

"All Fletchers are kin! You pick a fight with one and you might as well declare war on the state of Arkansas. The Ozarkies are full of them rifle-levering bastards!"

"Hawk, you're making a lot out of nothing."

"Could be, but where Fletchers are involved, nothing can be a whole lot. Wouldn't surprise me none if ol' Harlan wasn't on his way here."

"They ain't ghosts, Hawk."

"Maybe they ain't, but ol' Harlan enforces the law just by riding near a town!"

"Ain't they the ones who cleaned out Belmont down south?"

"Yeah. And they did it while riding through the damn place on their way to a Sunday social!"

Hawk watered the floor again. "Get the money. We're pulling out before we get hung."

"Where we going?"

"Texas maybe. We just might stop at ol' Harlan's place on the way. Sort of drop a hint that some of his kin are having it rough up here and are about to be hung. That'll teach Hollend to hang my friends!"

"We set foot on Fletcher's ranch and he'll bury us."

"Not if we go in with white flags tied to our rifle barrels. Get the money!"

They left. Sis wiped her forehead. "You suppose he really plans to see Uncle Harlan?"

"Whiskey talk. They're more apt to head north."

"We let day find us here, Jonah, and it's no telling what Sooey will do."

"Come into town screaming like a panther, is my guess."

"We'd better do something."

Footsteps paused at the door. It swung open. A woman came in and began opening a box.

"Henry!" Sis whispered.

She whirled around, eyes wide. "What are you two doing here?" she demanded in a hushed tone.

"We're locked in," Sis said.

Henry kept working at opening the box. "You're both crazy! Everyone is looking all over for you."

"Get the key and unlock the door," I said.

"The bartender keeps the key behind the bar," she told us,

removing two bottles from the box. "It'll take some doing, but I'll try."

"Try in a hurry," I pleaded.

She paused, her eyes searching mine. "Crazy fools. You're going to get yourself killed before I can realize my dream."

"What did she mean by that?" Sis wanted to know when Henry left.

"Some foolishness she thought up when she had the fever."

"She's not feverish now!"

"Don't 'pear to be."

Sis mumbled something and sat down to wait. A half hour passed. A chair slid abruptly against the floor. Then another. Yells went up and boots scraped the floor. A fist struck flesh. The saloon became a madhouse, with people scurrying every which way to escape fists and flying bottles.

Henry entered the storeroom. She partly closed the door behind her and rushed to the back, inserting a key into the padlock. It clicked open.

"I had to arrange for a fight in order to divert attention," she said. "Now, if I can just return the key."

"Forget that! You get out of the saloon and stay out," I said.

She left. I removed the padlock, and Sis and I slipped out the back, making sure the fuse was in place before closing the door.

Inside the saloon, it sounded as if others had joined the fight.

We moved quickly down behind the church house, darting under the steps to the back door.

It was a good place to hide. All we could do now was wait. Once, a rifle toter passed near the steps on his way to the street.

In the church house, activity slowed after a while. Young assignees began leaving as soon as the trade slackened. Most left by the rear door, hurrying down the steps and away. Several of the older women stayed, hoping, perhaps, to pick up any stragglers.

Eventually, the lamps went out and the last customer left with a woman steadying him toward a saloon. We moved from under the steps and tried the door. It didn't have a lock. Inside,

Sis checked behind the curtains while I placed the bundle of dynamite under the pew benches shoved against one wall.

"No one's here, Jonah."

I lit the fuse and followed her out the back. We ran across the open area to the rear of the nearest building.

It was slow going. We held close to the shadows, moving from the restaurant to the barber shop. When we neared the rear of the saloon, two men met at the alley up ahead, stopping to exchange complaints about having to do guard work. They lit cigarettes and moved on.

Crouching low, we made it to the saloon—just as the church exploded.

Those inside rushed to the street. Two guards appeared out of nowhere, running past us.

I lit the fuse and ran. Sis was on my heels as I turned the corner at the end building. We came up quickly. A guard at the livery stable was turning, searching the daybreak with his rifle.

"Get down there!" I shouted. "They need you. I'll watch this end!"

He bounded down the street.

The back half of the saloon lifted to the sky as Sis and I ran up the knoll. A rifle cracked. Then another. The bullets fell short, hitting at our heels. Several shouted for mounts as they ran toward the livery.

We found Sooey gesturing to the northwest and southwest. Riders approached fast from both directions. Both groups had seen us.

Below, in the corral, men were mounting up. We climbed into saddles. "Which way, Sis?"

She pointed straight west.

"We'll run right into them!"

"Not if our horses give it all they have," she yelled.

"It's suicide, Sis!"

She didn't hear me. Her stallion was already grabbing distance. I levered the Winchester as my horse jumped into motion. Sooey was out ahead of me.

# CHAPTER 15

WE raced against certain death. As soon as the two groups of riders realized our intentions, they turned to close the gap, whipping their horses.

They began shooting even though we were not yet in range. Sis and Sooey kept low. My horse reached hard for more ground, upset because he wasn't in front.

The ground ahead sloped lazily, the land a gentle arch over a wide span. As the distance shortened, more of them fired, bullets zapping close. I shouted in the stallion's ear for more speed.

The gap was closing fast. The three Winds seemed to know what was expected of them and they gave it all they had, pushing hard with hind legs.

It was going to be close. We'd passed the point of no return. Now, it remained all or nothing. I wanted to close my eyes. If a bullet found a target, I did not want to see it. Instead, I tried to aim for the lead horseman coming in on our right. It was impossible to hold a sight. I levered four quick shots at the bunch. One tumbled out of his saddle. Another's horse went down.

Swinging to the left, I relayed four or five shots at the group. A rider jerked awkwardly, grabbing for the saddlehorn. A horse stumbled and slowed to a hobble.

I shoved in new cartridges as we fled through the trap. Gunfire increased in angry bursts as they now hoped, at least, to keep us in sight.

Two moved out ahead of the others, good horses not to be outdone without a struggle. They came on, dropping back only slightly.

The lazy land dropped behind us as we neared the "hill country." At the top of a grade, we dismounted to rest the lathering horses. Soon, we saw the two riders crest a rise and come on. Farther back, the others must surely be following.

"Looks as if they intend riding us into the ground," Sis said, mounting.

We rode on, wondering how long they would push us. Later, coming to a narrow run of brush, we found water and paused to breathe the horses. A bullet hummed off a branch nearby. Up the incline, the two were outlined against a gray, cloudy sky.

Another bullet sang through the brush. The report of the rifle followed. "They can shoot," I said, knowing we'd better move before they found our range.

Riding out of their sight, we decided to risk a turn to the northwest, came upon a stream and followed it a short distance.

The stallions were tiring. Later, in the afternoon, we saw them farther back on the prairie, picking out our trail.

"How far would you say Morely's Settlement is from here, Jonah?"

"Six or seven miles, at least."

"We'll go there."

"You think we should? If they picked up fresh horses there, they'd surely catch up."

"Catching up is not what I'm thinking," she said.

"Whatcha mean?"

"I'm tired of running, Jonah. We can't be chasing all over Kansas running from two men!"

"They are persistent."

A whiff of cold wind brought a dampness to the air. We turned toward the settlement. Later, a slow drizzle settled in and we were soon riding wet.

Though it wasn't yet evening, lamps lit a few windows at the settlement. Supper cooked on a stove somewhere, filling the air with scents that made my belly growl. I suddenly realized we'd not eaten all day.

Five buildings, three small board-types and two of logs, were more or less evenly spaced about fifty feet apart along the road.

Morely's Trading Post was a large log building. We followed the cooking odors to the other log structure, which was a bar and restaurant with a blacksmith shop out in the back.

We found the smith under the shed repairing a wagon wheel. The heavy-built middle-aged man looked up briefly from his work.

"Grain's in the barn for the horses if you care to feed them. Ma's got stew on inside if it's yourself you be wanting to feed."

We fed the horses and went inside through the back door. The heat from the stove felt good and we lingered in front of it. On one wall, scrubbed pots and pans hung from an iron framework of hooks. On the other side, a fire ladder led up to a trap door in the roof.

The heat from the kitchen filled the front. Four small tables occupied one side of the room. The bar, three wide planks placed on saw horses, took up the other wall.

Rough sawn boards gave under our feet as we crossed to the rear table. Placing the cocked Winchester on the table, I pointed the barrel toward the front entrance.

Sis cocked the Colt, gently pushing it to the edge of the table. She covered it with her hat. Sooey, his ax across his lap, worried that the restaurant might be sold out of supper. The lamps, one centered on each wall, flickered from charred wicks, shedding poor light.

Ma, a plump, round-faced woman in her midforties, brought three large bowls of stew and returned to the kitchen for corn bread and apple pie.

"You want milk or coffee to drink?" she asked, when she returned.

"Milk," Sis said.

"Two glasses for me," Sooey said, grinning.

"Big fella like you needs more than that," Ma decided. She brought a full pitcher and set it near him.

The hot stew helped take away the chill. I watched the door, listening as I ate.

We finished eating. Ma brought us coffee, saying we needed something else hot if we were going to sit around in wet clothes.

We sipped coffee and waited. Outside, the drizzle turned to rain. When we were having our second cup, they came riding in.

The steady hammering on a steel wheel rim at the blacksmith shop stopped momentarily. The smith wasted no more time with them than he had with us.

I drew a long breath, slid my hand to the rifle, resting the top of my finger on the trigger. Sis picked up the Colt, holding it under the table.

Finally, the back door opened. Sis tensed, moving her gun to cover the kitchen door.

The smith mumbled something to his wife before coming into the room. He poured a drink behind the bar, gulping it down. "One be watching the front," he said bluntly. "One be under the shed watching the back door."

I put on my hat. "They plan to cut us down as soon as we step through a door," I said.

"What are we going to do, Jonah?" Sis was tired and unable to hide her fear.

"There's a way up to the roof."

She took my arm. "They might see you!"

"They might not."

Ma joined her husband behind the bar. He poured two drinks. I went to the kitchen, blew out the lamp, and climbed the ladder. The cold rain hit my face as the roof door ground open on rusty hinges.

Pulling myself out onto the roof, I tested the wood shingles. Being wet, they made little noise. They were slippery some, however.

I crawled toward the rear until I could see under the shed. All I could see was dark. Rain spattered off the roof into my face.

Finally, I detected movement behind the anvil. He had an

excellent position. The large section of tree trunk supporting the tool protected him completely. He stayed down, taking no chances.

I worked at loosening a shingle, keeping my eye on the anvil. It was a slow process. I dared not make a sound. All he had to do was look up and I'd be dead.

One end of the shingle came free as the rain switched to a flood. I felt myself slipping and held onto the shingle until I found a protruding nail head with the toe of my shoe. It held. I almost lost the rifle, though.

Freeing the shingle, I readied myself. I flipped the shingle hard toward the anvil. It caught the wind and slammed against the shed roof.

He was only a blur when he jumped up. Nevertheless, I fired. He stumbled around under the shed, groaning. I lay flat, the rain pounding my back. I silently worked the lever.

"You get 'em, Tate?" a voice yelled from a corner at the front.

The rain droned on the roof. "Hey! Tate?"

He moved along the side of the building toward the rear. Rain poured off the narrow eave, spattering onto his slicker.

He paused at the corner. "Tate?"

"I'm hit."

"You hold on. The others'll be here directly."

"It's bad."

"Where'd the shot come from, Tate?"

He mumbled something about pain. If others were coming, there was little time left. Gradually, I made it back to the trap door and slipped inside. I lowered the door carefully. Climbing down, I started toward the front. "Cover the back door," I told Sis.

Pulling the door open slowly, I went out. The one I hadn't shot stood against the rear corner, facing the shed. I moved quietly toward him, rifle ready. Halfway along, something—perhaps a noise I made or a sixth sense—told him I was there.

He swung around quickly, firing the rifle from his hip. The

bullet hit near my shoe. I fired back, but not from the hip.

He fell face down in a puddle. I ran past the corner to the shed. Tate lay on his back, both hands clamped against the bloody spot on his chest. He wasn't breathing too well.

At the back door, I called for Sis and Sooey. We led the stallions out of the barn. Horses were coming toward the settlement.

Our horses, though not completely rested, seemed ready to run. We encouraged them with a slap of the reins.

Once the settlement was behind us, we headed for our camp, the stallions slowing to an easy trot.

"They can't track us in this rain," Sis said.

It cleared up after a while. My injured arm pained some. It was noon before we reached the abandoned homestead, our clothes long ago dried by the hot sun. The stallions, as tired as we were, seemed irritable as we scouted for sign before riding in.

Little Hope's joke marshal, Henry, and Sweetie were waiting for us.

# CHAPTER 16

IN the barn, we slept through the afternoon. The aroma of boiling coffee awoke me. I also detected that flapjacks were about ready.

Sitting up quickly, I found myself looking directly into Sweetie's grinning jaws. His breath nearly choked me.

I spoke to him as kindly as I knew how. He snarled back as if I had insulted him. Using my elbows, I slid backwards over the straw until I was out of breath range.

Henry entered the barn, scolding the dog. In the brown riding skirt, white shirt, and black leather vest, she was downright pretty. She gently nudged Sweetie with the toe of her boot. He went over and lay down beside Sis, breathing in her face. She promptly sat up.

"Supper's about ready," Henry announced, loud enough to wake Sooey.

The fading light caught Henry's face. She smiled down at me, running fingers through her curls. "Did the bad ol' dog frighten Jonah?"

I tried to think of a suitable reply, but she was gone. I pulled on my shoes, noticing each sock had a big hole in it.

"Sis, both my socks have holes in them.

"So does the seat of your pants," she said, still grumpy over waking up to dog breath.

"Huh?"

I felt behind me. Sure enough, there was a rip in my britches. "Must have torn them while I was about to fall off that roof. Think you can fix it, Sis?"

"With what?"

"I can't go around like this!"

"You've underwear on."

"But that tear is in the same place as the slit in my longjohns!"

"Well, twist your britches around some then."

"Sis!"

She stood up, shaking straw out of her hair. "Don't be so modest, Jonah. Who cares if your rear is showing?"

"*I* care, that's who!"

She watched me from the corner of her eyes. "Actually, you don't have all that much back there to show."

"You wouldn't take it so lightly if it was your rear showing!"

She pulled on her hat, sticking her nose in the air. "Of course I wouldn't. I'm a full-grown woman."

She went out, slinging hair over a shoulder with a twist of her head.

I picked up the Winchester, twisted my britches sideways, and started out. Sooey, grinning, started to build up a slow conversation.

"Shut up, Sooey!"

Henry took a plate to the marshal sitting under the cottonwood. We filled ours and joined him. The badge looked no better out here than it did in town.

"Your pistol still empty?" I said.

His taut face remained hovered over his plate. The one eye, however, lifted to me, steady and searching. For the first time, I noticed the streaks of gray in his hair.

"It is, boy," he said simply.

"The old man send you out here?" Sis asked.

"He did."

"Why? Henry usually delivers his messages." She bit on a flapjack.

"Who knows why he does anything?" He chewed slowly. "You set any more dynamite and there won't be a town left."

"We don't plan blowing up anything else," Sis replied. "It's settling time now."

He chewed some more. "You could take Hollend Saturday night."

"Where?" I asked. "We haven't seen him or Smith lately."

"They seldom come to town anymore. They moved their headquarters out to the Lee place—you might know where it is—six miles out on the south road. A big log house."

"We've seen it," Sis said. "It's on a swell. More of a fort than a house."

"It's a fort," the marshal said. "No way you could get near that place unless you had an army."

"What about Saturday night?" she inquired.

"He'll be in the back room of Morely's Trading Post at the settlement. Seems he found a young thing over there he's fond of."

"He'd have a lot of men with him," I said.

"Last Saturday he had only Hawk with him," the marshal informed. "Hawk and a couple others have since left Little Hope."

Sis looked at me. I shrugged.

"Let's see. This is Thursday," Sis said, calculating.

"If we can take him there, it'll make things a lot easier," I offered.

She nodded. "What about Smith, Marshal? Did the old man say where we might get him?—away from the fort, I mean."

"He said when the Hollend thing was done, he'd contact you about Smith."

"Even if you find Hollend alone, it won't be easy," Henry said, pouring a fresh cup of coffee. "I've seen him use his gun."

"She's right," added the marshal. "He doesn't lie when he brags about how fast he is. He practices a lot too."

Sooey refilled his plate. I poured another cup of coffee. The moon peeked over the top of the trees. I finished my coffee and stood up.

Sis followed me over to the fire. "What do you think, Jonah? Should we give it a try Saturday night?"

"Let's think on it," I said. "Looks too easy somehow."

"That's what I was thinking." She sniffed in my direction. "Are you fixing to bathe?"

"I thought I would."

"Good," she said, and rejoined the others.

I found the lye soap and headed down to the stream, the Winchester over my shoulder.

Down a ways, between a growth of small cottonwoods, the stream deepened. There wasn't enough water to swim in, but we'd found it a good place to bathe.

I stripped, hung my clothes on a bush, and leaned the rifle in the fork of a branch. I moved out to where the water was just above my knees.

The flowing stream was cold. I soaped all over, dipped down, and soaped again. The moon gave fair light, even throwing shadows about.

I lay back in the water, enjoying the clean feeling while the running water washed away the soap.

It wasn't until I approached the bank for my clothes that I discovered Sweetie was lying there. When I started to leave the stream, he stood up, growling. I moved down a ways. He followed. When I went back, so did he. I started to get out anyway. He bared fangs and I decided I'd best not try it.

"You got a stupid name, you know that?"

He bristled up.

"Henry!" I called, it suddenly dawning on me that trickery was possible. "Henry? You there?"

"Uh huh" came the reply from behind a bush.

I rushed to the knee-deep water and dropped down. She came from behind the bush and sat on the bank, elbows on her knees, her chin resting in her hands.

"How long you been hiding behind that bush?"

"A long time."

"That ain't fair, Henry!"

"I know it."

"Give me my clothes."

She shook her head.

"Henry!"

"Ssshhh! They'll hear you."

"You'd better hand me my clothes."

"If I don't?"

"I'll come up there and sock you!"

"Come ahead."

I stayed where I was.

"You might as well come on out, Jonah. I've already seen you."

"You don't have a bit of manners!"

"Know something, Jonah? You're rather handsome—from the neck down."

"At least throw me my longjohns."

"Want to know what I dreamed about when I was feverish?"

"No."

"Then I guess I'll just sit here."

"I'll call Sis."

"Go ahead."

"Henry, this has gone far enough!"

"So, come on out."

"You're not going to pitch my longjohns to me?"

"No. If you want your old clothes, you'll have to come out and get them."

"I will after you leave with that dog."

"I'm not leaving."

I stood up. I figured the best way to get even with her was to show her I wasn't a coward. I walked out of the stream and over to my clothes, feeling stupid all the while.

"Well!" she said. "You're quite something, Jonah."

"Dammit, Henry!"

"Well, you are!"

I slipped on my longjohns quicklike. Standing up, she handed me the rest of my clothes. I put them on, too.

A slow smile parted her lips. "May I borrow your soap?" She began taking off her clothes.

"What are you doing?"

"I can't very well bathe otherwise, can I?"

I handed her the soap. "Would you mind staying, Jonah? I'd

hate to think I was down here all alone. You know, naked and all . . ."

I stayed. Pa'd said that if a pretty woman wanted to show a leg, a man was a fool not to look.

Henry waded out into the knee-deep water and began soaping. Beams of moonlight broke through the trees, sprinkling over her.

"*Jo-nah!*"

I jumped up.

"Shame on you!"

"That you, Sis?" Henry called from the stream as though she was asking for the correct time.

"Did you know Jonah was over here gaping at you?"

"*Gaping!* Jonah, you naughty boy!"

"Who? Me?"

"Henry!" Sis said, exasperated. "You might at least duck down or something."

"Tish, tosh," she said, soaping an underarm. "Jonah's not worldly. Besides, Sweetie will protect me."

"*You're* not the one I'm worried about!"

Henry giggled. Sis sighed. "Just don't stand there gawking, Jonah. Get on back to camp. I'd like to get a bath too sometime tonight."

"You didn't mind me looking at Jane," I said.

"That was for education; to relive your ignorance."

"So is this."

"Jonah!"

The coffeepot was still hot. I poured a cup and sat down near the marshal.

"You must have been real dirty," he reasoned.

"I was."

Sooey bit off a chew. When Sis and Henry came up, he took the soap and disappeared toward the stream.

"Never seen such a clean-minded bunch," the marshal offered.

"A little soap and water wouldn't hurt you," Sis told him pointedly.

"It ain't Saturday night," he said, working himself to standing with the aid of his crutches. "Think I'll get some sleep. Where'd you put my bedroll, Henry?"

"In the barn with mine."

"Get me up first light," he said, heading for the barn. "We need to get an early start back."

"Some say he used to be a fighter," Henry said, watching him entering the barn.

"Don't seem much now," I said.

"That's harsh, Jonah," said Sis.

"Guess I didn't mean that. I'm just not sure I trust him."

"The old man does," Henry said.

She looked at me, her eyes pulling some. "You trust me, don't you?"

I put a stick on the fire. "Not the least bit."

"Speaking of which," Sis said, matter of fact, "you two had better sleep at different ends of the barn tonight."

"Aw, tish, tosh, Sis!" She cast her eyes at me.

"I'm going to sleep under this tree," I said.

"Me, too," Henry replied quickly.

"So will I," Sis added firmly. She sipped on her coffee. "Jonah," she said after a while, "I've been thinking about Saturday night."

"We're going for Hollend?" I said.

She nodded, looking into the fire. "We need to finish it."

# CHAPTER 17

SATURDAY moved like a sick snail, filled with anxiety and uncertainty. I cleaned our guns, feeling tense. Every muscle seemed tight and uncoordinated.

It had all been building up over a period of time and I noticed Sis remained quiet, but she was jumpy, too. Sooey looked more concerned than usual, chewing and swallowing.

I never questioned the Fletcher way of righting wrongs. It was our father's way. It was the way of his father, and so far as I knew, it was a thing passed down from generation to generation.

What it came down to, you had to fight for the privilege of being left alone. You had to be ready to kill in order to live and ready to die to right a wrong.

The Fletcher way held that when someone robbed, cheated, killed, or violated a family member, it was the responsibility of the others to see that justice was properly rendered in a settlement.

*"You bury the son of a bitch!"* was Pa's way of expressing it.

We mounted up a little after sundown. Sis seemed to relax some once she was in the saddle. I believe I did too. A little.

We let the horses run off their energy and they settled down. Under different circumstances, it would have been a good night to ride. There was a moon and a comforting breeze.

"How are we going to do this, Sis?"

"Same as Pa would. You shoot it out in a draw-down—once we tell him why he's fixing to die."

I wished I had her confidence. "I ain't Pa, Sis."

"You're the head of what's left of this family, Jonah. You'll be acting in Pa's place."

"Pa was one of the best when it come to rifling. He would have been happy to face Hollend in a draw-down. Pa would have given him an equal chance or better."

"He gets equals, Jonah."

Frankly, I always felt that the Fletchers faulted in their generosity when it came to giving equals to killers. I said as much out loud.

"You can do it, Jonah," Sooey proclaimed, spitting.

A lot he knew.

"Sure he can," Sis tagged on. "Jonah just likes to short himself at times. With a little confidence, he could become a better rifler than Pa was."

If you weren't watchful, a Fletcher woman would put you in a root cellar occupied by two screaming cubs and a raging mama bear—or a big rattler.

"Hollend can't be all that good with a six-shooter, Jonah," she was saying.

"Yeah."

We dismounted on the grade northeast of Morely's Settlement. The only light was in the back room of the Trading Post. The weak cast of the moon released dim shadows about the buildings. Nothing stirred that we could tell. It was long past midnight.

We watched and waited, not really knowing what we were looking for. "Ready?" Sis asked after a while.

I breathed deeply. "I am if you are."

We went the rest of the way on foot, leading the horses. When we neared the Trading Post, I worked the Winchester's lever quietly, my heart beating in my throat. Nothing felt right.

A few feet from the building, we dropped reins, ground-tying the horses. They stood.

The thick curtain on the window prevented our seeing into the back room. We moved to the corner. Sis took a long, slow breath. "Cover us," she whispered. "We'll see if the door is locked."

"I still don't like this," I said in her ear.

She moved toward the door. Sooey followed, ax in hand. I dried my palms.

When she jerked open the door, all hell broke loose. Men, yelling, poured out of the room, knocking Sis down. One snatched the ax out of Sooey's hand as three others jumped on him. Men came running from the next building. I heard horses approaching from the direction of the blacksmith shop.

"Run, Jonah!" Sis screamed as two grabbed her.

Sooey swung his three assailants aside and hit one of the men holding Sis. It sounded as if his fist cracked a jaw. Others piled on him, swinging pistol butts.

I couldn't fire for fear of hitting Sis or Sooey. I ran. When my foot touched the stirrup, I yelled at the stallion. When he jumped, I almost lost my grip on the saddlehorn.

Hanging to the side of the running horse, I finally managed to swing a leg over, pulling myself into the saddle. Twice, I almost lost the rifle.

"Bring out the fast horses!" someone yelled.

When I looked back, Sooey was throwing men everywhere, screaming like a panther.

The other Winds followed close behind, stirrups swinging wild. Rifles cracked. I bent low.

Four riders were keeping up, firing as they came. I dug heels against Wind. He seemed to leap.

Up a hill, around another. They still kept up. Somewhere, they'd found four fast mounts and assigned lightweight men to ride them.

Later, coming to an almost flat stretch of prairie, I reined near one of the other stallions and switched over. When I hit the tip of the reins against his neck, he responded with a shake of his head and a grab for space. He was Sooey's horse, used to carrying a lot of weight.

The chasers, seeing the distance between us widen, fired almost steadily. The range would have been poor in daylight. At night, it was in my favor.

They intended catching me even if it meant riding their horses to death.

Thinking the worst about what might be happening to Sis and Sooey, I became angry. I slowed the stallion and turned toward a long, gentle slope. They saw the maneuver and cut across.

Over the top, I swung down and ran back to the crest, hitting the ground on my belly. Adjusting the rear sight, I made ready.

They started up. I gently squeezed the trigger. The first shot missed. I tried again. The lead rider fell backwards off his horse. The others came on, firing.

I sent another shot in their direction and ran for Sis's horse. I would be foolish to stay and take unnecessary risks while they held my sister and friend.

But I was no longer running from them. Not in the sense that I was trying to get away. I gave the stallion just enough rein to keep out of rifle range.

I would do it different this time. If I was lucky, I might get two of them.

The light was getting better. Day showed gently in the east. The rill ran along the bottom of two low swells.

Leaving the stallions behind a thicket to drink, I took position behind an old oak. It would be a long shot to the crest over which they had to ride. I set the sight accordingly.

Determined men sometimes do stupid things. These men did when they paused at the crest. I held the Winchester steady against the tree, slowly applying pressure to the trigger, not wanting to know at what point the hammer would fall.

I didn't know until the butt kicked my shoulder. The target slumped in the saddle, gradually falling to the ground.

The other two reined about, disappearing from the crest. I waited. They did not reappear.

When I rode up to the point, the two riders were moving toward Little Hope, their tired horses able to do no more than a slow trot.

They were out of range. Nevertheless, I felt like wasting a cartridge. The rifle cracked, the sound a long echo over the early-morning prairie. They looked back and began whipping their horses. The animals continued their tired, slow trot.

Searchers had been at our camp at the soddy. Everything of value was gone. Even the coffeepot and fry pan. What they hadn't taken they'd destroyed. Beans were scattered on the dirt floor. A half sack of flour emptied outside the door.

I ran to the barn, checking under the straw. The shotgun and dynamite were still there. Taking the stallions into the corral, I fed them what grain was left. I did not take off the saddles.

I had to think. Were they still alive? I felt empty. Alone. Beaten.

I really felt like crying. I didn't, however. If they were dead, there would be time enough for that later. Right now, I needed a plan.

When the horses finished eating, I hid one among the brush downcreek. Leaving one in the corral, I took the other with me upstream. If the hunters returned, I didn't want to be blocked from a horse.

Sitting on the bank, I must have thought of a dozen ways to rescue them—each of which would have resulted in our deaths.

It was near sundown when I heard the horse coming a ways off. When he crossed the stream, I stepped out from behind the tree, levering the Winchester, aiming at his middle.

"Hold it, boy!" shouted the old man, pulling up. Sweetie went into a crouch, ready to leap.

"I can kill you before that dog gets to me. I might even kill him, too!"

He snapped a finger. The dog sat.

"They used me, boy," he said. "I'll admit I was a fool to fall for it, but that doesn't change anything. They figured it out I was friendly to you three and was keeping in touch through Henry. They arranged for me to overhear the talk about Hollend being alone at Morely's Settlement."

I kept the rifle on him. "I never trusted you and I still don't, old man."

"If I were you, I wouldn't either."

"You've refused to say why you followed us here or what you intend doing. I think it's time you said."

"I told you, you'd know in due time. Until then, it's no concern of yours. Now, either shoot or point that rifle elsewhere! We got talking to do."

I uncocked. He rode on up to the soddy with Sweetie following. Taking a cloth sack out of the saddlebags, he limped over to the tree.

"Sit," he told me. "We'll eat these biscuits and chew jerky while we talk."

I sat down. He took a biscuit out and handed me the sack. "First off, your sister and friend are still alive."

"You saw them!"

"Yeah, I saw them. The girl is fine. Sooey has had the hell beat out of him. Clubbed with pistol butts, I'd say. Probably the only way they could subdue him."

"Where are they?"

"Locked up in the jail. Tomorrow at noon sharp, they'll be taken out, tied to a wagon wheel, and unless you show up, they'll be whipped to death. That's the message Hollend told me to give you."

"What happens when I show up?"

"He didn't say. You want my opinion?"

"He'll kill all of us by whip or gun."

"That's close. First, Smith will use his whip on each of you. Then Hollend will hang what's left, if anything."

"Maybe they'll let Sis go if I give up without a fight."

"Not likely. After what you three have done, they're not about to let either of you go."

"If the town knew I was trading myself for her, they might—"

"Forget it! What have I been saying all along, boy? There's not a man in that place who'd lift a finger to help. Hell, if Hollend should agree to release her, the people would prevent it. They want your blood. All of it! You've destroyed half the town and two thirds of the grazing around here."

I chewed on another biscuit.

"Matter of fact, you can expect everyone to turn out tomorrow to enjoy the whipping and hanging," he said bluntly.

"You, too?"

He ignored that. "If you're thinking about trying to break them out of jail, forget it. There's a dozen armed men guarding them. Hollend said any attempt on the jail and he'll burn it down with them in it."

The silence hung heavy. The jerky tasted flat.

"Where's Henry?" I asked.

"I sent her away where she'd be safe."

He stood up, looking down on me. "You could get on one of those stallions and put Kansas behind you. You don't have to ride in there tomorrow to die."

"When I leave Kansas, my sister and Sooey will be with me." I came to my feet. "Will you take two of the horses back with you?"

He nodded. I went to gather them. When I returned, he mounted and took their reins. "They'll be at the livery." He looked around. "Look, boy. You got a plan at all?"

"Of sorts. If we die, we'll not be the only ones."

# CHAPTER 18

I cut off a two-foot section of a branch and trimmed it to fit snugly down the left barrel of the shotgun. Going to the barn, I carefully wrapped the ten sticks of dynamite into a tight bundle around one end of the stick and tested the fit again.

The bundle held close against the end of the barrels even when I pointed the shotgun toward the ground.

I put a handful of double-aught shells in my coat pocket, slid a shell into the right barrel of the gun, and snapped it shut.

Earlier, I test-fired each barrel twice, not wishing to leave anything to chance. I slid the fully loaded Winchester into the saddle scabbard and mounted up.

I rode holding the dynamite-loaded double-barrel against my legs. I had only to snap back the right hammer and pull the trigger and that would be the end of me and everything within a wide circle.

When I approached Little Hope, the sun was at the noon point.

Entering the town, I reined up. I shifted the butt of the gun to rest on my hip, barrels up. I pulled the right hammer back, the metallic click sounding loud. Those standing in the street quickly moved onto the walks. I slid my finger through the brass guard, resting it on the trigger.

A murmur arose as word spread along the street. Everyone stepped back farther. Most were holding guns. One fool raised a rifle toward me. The cowboy standing at his elbow knocked it down, cursing him.

I pulled down my wide-brim, holding the reins tight. The stallion did not know how to walk straight ahead. He snorted, jerking his head up, neck arched, and pranced sideways down the street toward the wagon at the other end of town.

Those around the wagon moved back quickly as word reached them. They spread out in a semicircle. Sooey was tied to the rear wheel, his back against the hub. It looked like Smith planned to tear out his eyes with the first blows.

His face was swollen and blue with bruises. Dried blood matted streaks through his hair. He must have put up one hell of a fight.

Sis's back was exposed bare to the glaring noonday sun. Her black hair shone even though covered with dirt. She was naked down to her waist.

They'd moved a table to the center of the street, putting it up at the end of the wagon tongue. It was covered with a white cloth. Bottles and glasses were neatly arranged in the center.

Smith and Hollend sat at the table, not knowing whether to shoot or run. All of Little Hope had intended to make it a party. Now that it had started, they were having doubts.

The whip was neatly coiled on the table in front of Smith. He toyed with the handle nervously. As I neared, he and Hollend stood up slowly. Hollend removed his pin-striped coat. The cut-down holster was tied down. Small unblinking eyes gazed out from under his hat. I noticed he had to swallow.

The stallion edged closer to the table, blowing. They started to move back.

"Take another step backwards and they'll be picking up your pieces in Texas!" I warned.

"Kill them, Jonah!" Sis yelled.

The short bartender, who was standing near her, had been wiping his hands on the apron strung around his bulge. He reached a hand around her, grabbed a breast and squeezed. Sis managed to stifle a scream.

My eyes followed him as he moved to the porch of the barber shop. The slanted grin stayed on his face.

"You pull that trigger and we all go up!" Hollend said quickly.

"That's my opinion too," I replied, glad I was able to keep tremors out of my voice.

"Your sister and friend would be killed with the rest of us!"

"We came here prepared for that."

"You be careful now," said Hollend. "Let's talk this out."

"Here's how it'll be," I said. "Cut them loose. We ride out of here, slowlike, you and Smith walking in front of our horses."

"Then what?"

"That's the part we'll talk about when we're away from this crowd."

A cowboy at the edge of the onlookers raised his rifle.

"You damn fool!" yelled Hollend. "You'll get us all killed! Somebody take that gun away from him."

People started edging back. "Hollend." My mouth was dry. "Better tell them to stand pat. They're all in this thing. If anyone tries to leave, I pull this trigger. I won't be giving a second warning."

"Don't nobody move, dammit!"

My heart raced. I tried to wet my lips, but my tongue was too dry. Silence hung like death's breath over the street. Hollend was weighing it all. Each second was like a minute. He measured me slowly, perhaps wondering whether he could draw and fire before I had time to jerk the trigger and blow the whole place sky-high.

Hollend nodded to the two men standing near the wagon. They drew pistols, holding them cocked to Sis's and Sooey's heads.

"Could be you're bluffing, boy," Hollend said, his voice tight.

"Try me."

He shifted his weight. Smith's stubby fingers tensed around the whip handle, milking it. Hollend's eyes ran over the crowd along the street and then back to me. His hand was close to his gun, fingers stretching. He was apparently still trying to sort out the odds.

He grinned nervously. "You got yourself a problem, boy." A thin cackle came from his tight throat.

"That's true enough. But you've a bigger one. I know what I'm going to do and when I'm going to do it."

He sat down abruptly and poured a whiskey. Bringing the glass to his lips, he tasted it slowly. The hand was steady.

"We'll wait," he said. "You're not going to pull that trigger without cause. We'll wait."

A drop of sweat fell off my nose.

"Jonah." Sis called weakly.

"Katrina?"

"Wait five minutes, Jonah. No longer. Understand?"

"Five minutes," I said. "Unless someone tries to leave."

No one did. The sun seemed hotter. Not even a breeze stirred. Hollend poured another drink. Some of the steel was gone from his hand. Smith's roundish face glistened with perspiration.

The stallion stomped, and snorted. I tightened the reins.

"Only three minutes more, Jonah," Sis reminded after a while.

Sooey lifted his head, looking at me. One of his eyes was swollen shut. "We gonna win, Jonah?"

"We're going to win, Sooey,"

"We die, though, huh?"

"Maybe."

"It all right, Jonah. Long as we win."

"Two minutes, Jonah," Sis said a little later.

The man standing over her shoved the pistol barrel hard against the back of her head. "Shut up!" he ordered. "Shut up, dammit!"

"One minute," I said loudly.

They came in at the other end of town, walking their horses. Uncle Harlan was out in front. Five of his sons spaced themselves the width of the street. Behind them rode the other two, in the middle of the street, sitting backwards in their saddles, protecting their backs.

Uncle Harlan levered. Then each of my cousins levered in turn, slowly, deliberately. Uncle Harlan swung the rifle barrel across his right shoulder. His sons did likewise. Their rifles were .44 Winchesters. Their fingers were set to trigger.

They came on, slowly. Quick Fletcher eyes searched from under each black wide-brim. All wore chaps and working spurs. Their mounts were lathered and dusty. They'd ridden hard.

Uncle Harlan's long black coat was open in front, and his tall, thin frame sat erect. Fixed jaw and straight mouth, he looked directly ahead, except for the one time he turned to look where the bank had been.

Each of his boys wore vests—not the fancy kind, but those designed for hard service. The one who chewed tobacco was on Uncle Harlan's left, near the walk. He turned his head and spat, the stream hitting a townsman's pants leg and boots. David—or was it Solomon?—didn't give a damn for nothing.

Uncle Harlan kneed his horse to a halt about twenty feet from me. His sons reined up, still in position.

My uncle looked to where the two men held cocked pistols on Sis and Sooey. His eyes then traveled to Marvin Hollend and Oates Smith. He grunted.

Turning his head toward me, he gave the bundle of dynamite and cocked shotgun due scrutiny.

"Stand steady, boy," he advised as the stallion stomped and blew.

Slowly, he took it all in again. Twisting in the saddle, he looked back along the walks, at Sis, at Sooey, at those behind the table.

His eyes came back to me. My tobacco-chewing cousin spat on another pair of boots.

"What you have here, Jonah, is what folks in Arkansas call an 'Ozarks social.'"

"I've heard of such."

He loaned his attention to the two men standing over Sis and Sooey. "Jeremiah? David?"

"Yeah, Pa?"

"If they don't uncock and leather in due course, put it between their eyes!"

"Sure thing, Pa."

They uncocked and leathered.

"Now cut them loose!" he ordered the two men.

They did that, too.

"Katrina," he called out. "What's passed, baby? Aside from what I see, they violate you?"

"Just some feeling, pawing, and slapping, Uncle Harlan," she said, pulling on her shirt.

"Point out the sons of bitches!"

She finished with the shirt buttons and turned around. She pointed to the aproned bartender in front of the barber shop.

He started to run. Uncle Harlan shot him in the temple. With a twist of his wrist, he flipped the rifle down and up, levering one-hand fashion.

He took his time searching the scene again. His gaze fell back to those at the table.

"All right! Where's the bastard who's going to get this social underway? Let him step forward! I don't intend sitting out here in this hot sun all day!"

No one moved.

"Boys," he said turning in the saddle. "In due course, shoot any son of a bitch holding or wearing iron!"

They said they would.

Guns fell to the walks and street. Hollend started to unbuckle.

"Keep yours," I said.

Uncle Harlan turned to me. "Get on with it, Jonah."

I eased the hammer to safety, removed the bundle of dynamite, and pitched it to Luke. He made a right smart catch.

Dismounting, I broke open the shotgun, shoved a shell in the empty barrel, and snapped the gun closed. I cocked both hammers and handed it to Sis. "If Smith moves, kill him!"

I pulled the Winchester from its scabbard and walked to the middle of the street. Facing the table, I wiped a sleeve over my forehead. My legs felt weak and trembly.

"What's it to be, boy?" Uncle Harlan said.

"Draw-down," I said, levering and swinging the barrel to shoulder. "With Marvin Hollend."

"Let one Marvin Hollend step out!"

He moved from behind the table. My chewing cousin spat. A woman started to protest.

Hollend positioned himself, feet apart, long fingers stretching near the pistol butt. "When I kill a man—or boy—I like to know why he's dying."

"Tell him, Sis," I said, not trusting my voice. I watched his eyes.

She told him, her voice slow, even.

"I see," he said flatly. He looked up at Uncle Harlan. "After I kill him, what then?"

Uncle Harlan turned in his saddle. "Matthew? Luke?"

"Yeah, Pa?"

"*If* he wins, give him one hour's head start and then hunt him down and hang him!"

"Right, Pa."

"And, Matthew?"

"Yeah, Pa?"

"Don't you and your brother come home until it's done."

"We won't, Pa."

He turned back to Hollend. "Anything else?"

"I'm good at this sort of thing," he said. "The boy is as good as dead. You know it. He knows it."

Uncle Harlan grunted. "That aside, see to your own funeral arrangements—just in case. We Fletchers ain't undertakers! Anything else on your mind?"

"Yeah. Get ready to bury kin!"

"One thing you might not know, gunfighter!" snapped Uncle Harlan. "Fletcher boys come into the world levering Winchesters. Their first cries are for ca'tridges—not titty!"

Hollend gave me all his attention. His eyes searched for a weakness. I wondered if he suspected my legs were on the verge of shaking.

"Compared to me, ol' Soltz was slow, boy!" He grinned. He was still looking for a weakness, not completely sure how fast I could bring the rifle down.

I swallowed. "*Jonah.*" It was Pa's voice I heard, coming to me from out of the past. "*In a draw-down, focus on the spot you want your bullet to hit. Stare at that place. Keep the whole man in view, but concentrate on that one small area. Concentrate, Jonah. Concentrate. Tell your brain to order every muscle to deliver speed. Forget about everything else! Focus and believe. When you bring the rifle down, it'll already be aimed. The bullet will strike that spot. If you're any good, it will be dead center.*"

Hollend moved. The gun cleared the cutaway, but that was all. The spot in the center of his chest exploded, knocking him back against the wagon. His legs trembled violently. His eyes grew wide in disbelief.

The second bullet opened his throat. I turned to Smith, levering.

"He's mine!" The old man pushed his way through the crowd on the walk and limped out into the street, that devil of a dog stalking behind him.

# CHAPTER 19

THE old man held the long double-barrel cocked and ready.

"State your reason," Uncle Harlan told him.

"He whipped my daughter to death!"

My uncle turned to me. "Jonah?"

I uncocked. "He's yours, old man."

He turned to face Oates Smith. "I was there right after you left," he said, his voice strained. "You followed her from room to room, popping that whip to her face and body!"

He broke off quickly, his voice choking. "Couldn't you see that she was about ready to give birth?"

The muscles along Smith's short neck twitched. Sweat popped out on his face. He rapidly milked the whip handle.

"Recognize the dog?" the old man continued. "He belonged to her. He was just a puppy then. You cut him up bad with your whip too. But he lived."

"Don't you sic that dog on me!" Smith cried.

"Why not? You have your whip. How good are you with that thing when your victim isn't a woman, a bound man, or a puppy?"

"Keep that dog away from me!" he whined, dropping the whip handle.

"He recognizes you. I'm sure he does. Look at his fangs! He remembers, all right."

Sweetie appeared ready to leap, the hair along his back straight up, ears folded back.

"Pick up the whip," ordered the old man, pointing the shotgun at Smith's roll of a belly.

Smith grabbed the whip.

"Now, walk to the livery."

"You can't do this!"

"Who's going to stop me? It's settlement time. Now, get over there! Who knows, maybe you can make friends with the dog."

Nearing the livery, Smith broke into a run. He dashed inside and tried to close the door. It was too late. Sweetie leaped inside.

The whip cracked. Sweetie growled. Again the whip cracked. And again. Then there was such snarling, growling, whip popping, and screaming as you never heard. Shortly, it was mostly screaming.

After a while, the dog came out. The old man limped over to his horse and climbed into saddle. He reined over to us.

"I used you three. It was the only way I knew to get Smith in a public settlement. When I heard about what happened at Timber Creek last year, I got me this idea. Keep the stallions. You earned them."

He rode out of town with the dog following.

It was cool inside the small saloon. My cousins were seated about, and Uncle Harlan stood at the bar having a short whiskey with Sis. Sooey and I sipped our soda pop. We were relaxing before pulling out.

The marshal came in and ordered whiskey at the end of the bar.

"Jonah!" Sis cried sharply.

I turned. My rifle was on the bar. Gage was standing just inside the door, the cocked rifle pointed at me.

"Know'd I'd find you. Just know'd it!"

The marshal turned on his crutches. "Put it down!" his thin voice demanded.

Gage laughed. "Well, I heard about you, crip. Know all about you and that empty pistol you tote!"

The marshal pulled the Colt, cocking. "I said put it away. If there's to be any more killing in this town, the law'll do it!"

Laughing, Gage swung the rifle on him. "Think I'll call your bluff, crip."

The marshal pulled the trigger. The .45 roared, the bullet taking Gage through the door.

"Well," Uncle Harlan said. "Looks like a parcel of law and order has returned to this hell hole."

The marshal downed his whiskey. "You're damn right it has," he mumbled, going out.

Out of the corner of my eye, I saw Luke over at a table ease down the hammer of his Winchester. The tobacco-chewer, at the rear of the saloon, spat across the table and did likewise.

They all finished their whiskies and lit cigars. "Let's ride, boys," Uncle Harlan said. "We've cattle to work."

We mounted up, Sis, Sooey, and me on the three Winds.

"Boy," Uncle Harlan said, "when we get to home, you have a little redhead to tame. Daniel, what was that message Jane-gal wanted me to pass to Jonah?"

"I forget, Pa. Some nonsense about swans."

"I'll see you all there!" I shouted, kicking heels against the stallion and holding onto my wide-brim.